Hunk City

May 1, '07

To June,

With real admiration for a talented writer with a great future ahead of her!

All best,

ALSO BY JAMES WILCOX

*Heavenly Days*
*Plain and Normal*
*Guest of a Sinner*
*Polite Sex*
*Sort of Rich*
*Miss Undine's Living Room*
*North Gladiola*
*Modern Baptists*

# Hunk City

A NOVEL

James Wilcox

*[signature: James Wilcox]*

Viking

VIKING
Published by the Penguin Group
Penguin Group (USA) Inc., 375 Hudson Street, New York, New York 10014, U.S.A.
Penguin Group (Canada), 90 Eglinton Avenue East, Suite 700, Toronto, Ontario,
Canada M4P 2Y3 (a division of Pearson Penguin Canada Inc.)
Penguin Books Ltd, 80 Strand, London WC2R 0RL, England
Penguin Ireland, 25 St. Stephen's Green, Dublin 2, Ireland (a division of Penguin Books Ltd)
Penguin Books Australia Ltd, 250 Camberwell Road, Camberwell, Victoria 3124, Australia
(a division of Pearson Australia Group Pty Ltd)
Penguin Books India Pvt Ltd, 11 Community Centre, Panchsheel Park, New Delhi - 110 017, India
Penguin Group (NZ), Cnr Airborne and Rosedale Roads, Albany, Auckland 1310,
New Zealand (a division of Pearson New Zealand Ltd)
Penguin Books (South Africa) (Pty) Ltd, 24 Sturdee Avenue, Rosebank,
Johannesburg 2196, South Africa

Penguin Books Ltd, Registered Offices: 80 Strand, London WC2R 0RL, England

First published in 2007 by Viking Penguin, a member of Penguin Group (USA) Inc.

10 9 8 7 6 5 4 3 2 1

Copyright © James Wilcox, 2007
All rights reserved

PUBLISHER'S NOTE. This is a work of fiction. Names, characters, places, and incidents either are
the product of the author's imagination or are used fictitiously, and any resemblance to actual
persons, living or dead, business establishments, events, or locales is entirely coincidental.

LIBRARY OF CONGRESS CATALOGING–IN–PUBLICATION DATA
ISBN 978-0-670-03152-8

Printed in the United States of America

*"It is a law of the natural universe that no being can exist on its own resources. Everyone, everything, is hopelessly indebted to everyone and everything else."*

—C. S. Lewis

# Part One

## An Offer

*D*espite the sign, Redds Dollar Store is not "Open Roun'da Clock." When Burma Van Buren, née LaSteele, tried to peel the smiling clock from the entrance, she was demoted from manager to assistant manager of the bargain store. That's what you get for being honest. Redds actually closes every evening around six and doesn't reopen until nine in the morning—sometimes as late as nine-thirty if Miss Brown is moody and won't go out to relieve herself in the sweet olive. All this about Miss Brown, her mother's shih tzu, Burma explained in an e-mail to management. But they said corporate policy forbade any signatory deletion from a Class D franchise without an exclusion from Article XV. Besides, they added, "Roun'da Clock" doesn't mean *literally* open twenty-four hours a day. "We grow the wordage to mean that some A.M. and P.M. hours are hopefully impacted."

"Me, I would've quit so fast it'd make your head spin," Burma's accountant told her.

Mr. Harper, the accountant, is one of the worst Republicans imaginable, a *young* Republican. Normally, even though she is a Christian and is supposed to hate the sin but love the sinner, Burma wouldn't go near a Republican with a ten-foot pole. But she's reluctant to fire Mr. Harper, who was her late husband's accountant. It's not just a matter of hurting his feelings, although this is a factor, since he's so young, only in his mid-forties, and sensitive about his looks. He's sort of pretty, you see, and certain clients have been known to ask him out for a mocha latte because of his long lashes.

No, the main reason Burma doesn't fire Mr. Harper is that he's the executor of the estate, and a resentful executor would only make matters worse. As it is, Burma is spending far too much time signing papers she can't even pretend to understand and fending off count- less charities. Her late husband had been a catfish farmer who won the Pick Twelve lottery. After a string of jury trials contesting the will—three ex-wives and their assorted grandchildren, thirty-two of them, had sued her—Burma is rumored to be as rich as Denny, the man who founded Denny's. Yet her assets as of June 28, the day of Mr. Harper's visit, were only $36,497,682.47—minus the lawyers' fees, which were still being contested. Two of the ex-wives had passed away from old age during the trials, and Mr. Harper didn't think it was fair the lawyers should claim their victory fees, especially after one of the grandchildren had pulled out a .38 on the witness stand and, screaming, *White trash whore!,* accidentally shot her own foot instead of Burma, who felt so sorry for her that she gave this unhinged and untenured assistant professor of mass communication a lifetime annuity, much to Mr. Harper's disgust.

"Yes, sir," the accountant went on during this visit to Burma's mother's home, "I would quit that place so quick . . ." He snapped his fingers at the Redds calendar hanging above the toaster. "Make your head spin."

"I *can't* quit, Mr. Harper." Burma took a bite of the sandwich her mother had made for her, headcheese in a low-carb pita pocket. "They haven't found a replacement for me yet."

"That's Redds's problem. Not yours."

How many times had she tried to explain to Mr. Harper that there were such things in life as loyalty and duty? Burma's first job out of col- lege had been at Redds, back when it was called Sonny Boy. Yes, she'd been working at the very same store since May 17, 1971, the day she turned in her final paper at St. Jude State College, six pages on *As I Lay Dying*. It was an A+ paper, and she could have gone on to grad school if she didn't hate writing so much. They ever had a Ph.D. with all multiple choice, Mr. Harper would be calling her *Dr.* Van Buren now.

" 'Course I want to move out of here," Burma said, prompted by a remark of his after he banged his head on the ceiling. The low ceilings suited her mother just fine. Unlike her daughter, Mrs. LaSteele was so compact that even the 6×7 kitchen seemed roomy to her.

"You think a fifty-seven-year-old woman enjoys living with her mother?" Burma went on after Mr. Harper settled back down onto the dinette chair. Miss Brown had startled Mr. Harper when she sulked into the kitchen and nipped his leg.

"That means she likes you," Burma reassured the accountant, who was peering under the table for the dog. "Miss Brown only bites people she likes."

"Well, in any case," he said, fingering his calf, "you ought to be moving out of here soon enough. I got you an offer."

"Someone's going to buy Graceland?"

"We're going to unload it, Miss Burma. All you got to do is . . ."

As he rummaged through his briefcase, Burma chewed thoughtfully on the pita. Graceland II, which she had moved out of even before her husband had died, was a replica of Elvis's house, only much bigger. Mr. Van Buren had built it on his catfish farm after winning the lottery. The house had a lot of bad memories for Burma—not the least of which was Elvis himself. She and Mr. Van Buren had often quarreled over the merits of Elvis—and once he had run over her bare toes in his golf cart after she declared that Elvis was a symbol of everything that was wrong with this country. Why don't you build a replica of Stravinsky's house? she had demanded. Or Ralph Nader's? Why must you worship some bloated addict who . . .

5

"It's a consortium, not a person," Mr. Harper explained once he had found the papers. "A consortium wants it."

"How much are they offering?"

"Seventeen percent of the gate, plus two-point-three incentive points in tax abatement."

Burma had to ask Mr. Harper to repeat this. Her mind had wandered to that client of his who had drained a whole bottle of DayQuil because Mr. Harper refused a second cup of latte at the Starbucks in Piggy Wiggly. To think Mr. Harper—pretty, yes, but bland as all get out, and sort of slow, too, always getting his 6's mixed up with his 9's—to think that a man like him could inspire such passion . . .

"Estimated three-two a year in box office receipts?" she asked after he explained what gate meant. "Receipts for what?"

Mr. Harper adjusted a strand of his salt-and-pepper hairdo with an unusually long index finger. Pat Buchanan was what the client with a cold thought he looked like, sort of a cross between Pat Buchanan and Salma Hayek.

"I don't understand a thing you're saying," Burma finally broke in after Mr. Harper went on and on about amortization. "Just how much will I get for the place? Make it simple. Two million, three?"

"Possibly, considering the tax breaks."

"In other words, I'm going to give the place away for nothing? Is that it?"

"No, Miss Burma. The historic trust will make sure you realize a certain income from the productions, which over time . . ."

"What productions?"

After peering under the table again, he said, "You realize your husband's catfish farm is on a historical site? Yes, ma'am, the first prison ever built in the Florida Parishes stood right where Pond A25 is located. AmStar Historic Trust will duplicate the compound with every detail guaranteed authentic, down to the shoelaces of the guards. They want to convert Graceland II into a museum and IMAX. I guarantee you'll have schoolchildren from the tristate area just begging to get in."

"Hold on." Burma snapped a rubber band on her wrist. "There's no way on God's green earth I'm going to allow my property to be turned into a fake prison. No, sir."

Mr. Harper smiled. Yes, there was something vaguely dreamy about the smile—so boyish and innocent it almost made you forget his politics.

"Hear me out, Miss Burma. You'll be doing yourself a big favor by coming aboard. Look, the house has been on the market for almost a year. Nobody wants to live way out there. It's in the wrong school district. I've crunched the numbers, and believe me, by giving it to AmStar, you're doing yourself a big favor. First off, you get a gold star for being the biggest oleomysonary this town's ever known. At the same time you'll be saving yourself a bundle. Don't you realize that in your tax bracket, you've *got* to give to worthy causes or the government won't leave you enough to pick your titties with?"

That was another mistake he was always making, calling teeth "titties." Burma slid the dinette chair back to stretch her aching legs.

"Who was locked up in that prison anyway?"

"The scum of the earth, Miss Burma. Traitors. Men who refused to fight."

"Fight what?"

"The Spanish. They refused to fight for independence from Spain. See, St. Jude Parish here was its own country for a while, an independent republic along with Tangipahoa, Livingston, all the parishes east of the Mississippi that didn't get sold to the United States by Napoleon. We weren't part of the Louisiana Purchase, you know."

Her brow furrowed, Burma whisked some crumbs off the vinyl

tablecloth. "How can you have an IMAX of people refusing to fight? Who's going to pay to see that?"

Mr. Harper chuckled. "That's not your worry, young lady. Now, all I need is your John Hancock here, here, and here. That'll do for today."

With a groan, Burma levered herself from the table and tossed her plastic plate into a scented trash bag.

"Look, they only give me forty minutes for lunch, Mr. Harper. Don't get me all upset when I'm supposed to be digesting."

"Later, then."

"You get me a normal buyer. That's all I want, someone normal who just wants to live there in peace without any authentic shoelaces strutting around. No, I don't want to hear anymore about it, darling—uh, Mr. Harper. That's it."

## Tea at Redds

*A*t four that afternoon Burma filled the electric pot with tap water from the sink. She watched the pot so steadily, her mind elsewhere, that she didn't even realize when the water began to boil. As a matter of fact, ever since she'd become a person of substance, her mind was often elsewhere. More than once she wandered about the supply room at Redds, forgetting what she had come in for.

Nothing seemed right to her anymore. If it weren't for Mr. Harper—and the lawyers' bills—she would have let those goddamn grandchildren have every last cent. Lord knows it wasn't worth it, being called trash in a public courtroom, a cheap gold digger, a whore, after all the backbreaking work she had done to improve her mind. Does trash take night classes at St. Jude in music appreciation? Does a cheap gold digger ride to work each morning listening to *The Way We Live Now?* I ask you, how many whores put the parental lock on Bill O'Reilly to teach their mama some manners?

Yes, even though Burma had been brought up without any advantages, dirt poor, with a mama who had sprayed Lysol all over her copy of *As I Lay Dying,* it was so dirty, Burma had never given up. She got her A+. And if it was the last thing she did, she was going to get through the entire Trollope novel if it killed her.

"Shall I pour?"

It was Mr. Pickens, the superintendent of Streets, Parks, and Sewers. Four o'clock tea had been his idea. He was the one who had given her the two china cups for her sixty-first birthday—Lenox Solitaire from the mall in Mississippi. Why in the world had she ever accepted them? If she had an ounce of sense, she'd give them back.

"One lump or two, Burma?"

He plopped the cubes into her Darjeeling with silver tongs, also a gift, but this one from his wife. Mrs. Pickens had thrown a bridal shower for Burma, back when she was about to marry Mr. Van Buren, who was then, prelottery, just a catfish farmer, and nearly bankrupt. That would be the last time Burma ever married someone because she felt sorry for him. Twenty-six years older than her, that's what Mr. Van Buren had been. She had met him in a chat room, where if he didn't exactly lie about his age, he certainly used a much younger photo. Burma herself was fifty-something then, but everyone had said she looked ten or fifteen years younger, which was why her mother felt justified in posting her daughter's age online as thirty-five. (Burma's mother was the one who had surfed into the chat room and initiated a few conversations in Burma's name. The thought of having a daughter reach sixty and still not manage to reel

9

in a husband was too much for Mrs. LaSteele. It reflected so badly on Burma's upbringing.)

If Mr. Pickens hadn't gone and got himself married, Burma probably wouldn't have agreed to marry an eighty-year-old, no matter how many free catfish she would have gotten. She'd show Pickens that two could play that game.

"Why must you ask me that every time, Bobby Pickens? You know I take three lumps."

"I know, but I'm always hoping you'll see that I'm right. Two is plenty."

The office they were fussing about in used to be Mr. Pickens's. Back in the seventies, when he had been assistant manager of Redds—or rather, Sonny Boy—Burma had been a senior clerk. And had had the misfortune to fall in love with him. Nothing had ever come of it, though, besides a few tepid dates she herself had initiated. Mr. Pickens was married now to a woman who worked across the tracks at WaistWatch, which was why he had to sneak in the back door of Redds for high tea. His wife was extremely suspicious, even though there was nothing at all for her to worry about, at least as far as Burma herself was concerned. Mr. Pickens, you see, had become a Republican. He had started out a Democrat and then switched sides in order to run for superintendent of Streets, Parks, and Sewers.

"Here's your book," he said, handing over the Molly Ivins she had given him a month ago.

"Did you even bother to open it?"

"Look, I've got meetings coming out the wazoo. Plus, First Baptist expects me to run the small-arms auction for the new organ, and I'm not, I just am not."

As he steeped the Fortnum & Mason in a tea ball, she perused him sadly. Something was missing. The pocket protector he used to wear, brimming with Bics? Yes, but it wasn't just his clothes now, the snazzy way his wife outfitted him. It was his eyes—that lost look he used to have. Where was it? Why did he have to look so smug and complacent these days?

"Enough, Bobby." This she said more than once during the next half hour. He was nagging her again about her mother's home.

"Here you are, rich as a coot, and you're still living in that dollhouse with your mama," he went on. "People are beginning to talk, Burma."

"What business is it of theirs? This is a free country, isn't it?"

"Yeah, but you got that great big mansion just sitting out there, doing nothing."

"How many times I told you I hate Elvis? Besides, it'd take me plum near a half hour to get to work everyday."

Mr. Pickens smoothed the Microtex self-cleaning tie she had given him as a wedding present. "All right. I got just the thing for you. The old Dambar place, it's not five minutes away. You could even walk to work."

"You crazy? What would I want with thirty rooms to keep clean?"

"It's only twenty-two."

"I've already got a bushel of rooms at Graceland going to waste."

"That's why you should let AmStar have it, Burma."

"You been talking to Mr. Harper? How come he's blabbing to you about my private affairs?"

She was rinsing the teapot in the janitor's sink, one of the perks of the assistant manager's office.

"I was the one who suggested it to him. Burma, this is going to put Tula Springs on the map. Tourists will come from all over."

"For what? No one cares that some guys decided not to fight the Spanish way back."

"You kidding? What if the Spanish had won? Tula Springs would be a part of Cuba now. We might all be under Castro and forced to learn Spanish."

The lawn chair he was sitting in squeaked as he crossed his legs. For a moment she was afraid the frail aluminum might fold under his well-nourished heinie.

"Besides, do you realize what the tax revenue on an IMAX would bring in?"

"Graceland isn't even in the city limits."

"We're redrawing the boundaries, Burma, just for you."

"Get out of here, Bobby. Go back to work. I got me a customer."

"No, hon, these clothespins aren't on sale. They're ninety-eight cents, just like it says."

The woman sniffed the label suspiciously. "Y'all got par'kee seed? I used to buy all my seed here—right yonder." Her turbaned head nodded toward the aisle where Sonny Boy had sold birdseed fifteen years ago. But Redds, Burma explained, no longer carried any.

"Why you stop sellin'?" Ralph Lauren was blazoned across the massive front of her T-shirt. "I need that for my care package, some of that seed. She like them clothespins, too."

Though the customer didn't seem that old, late forties perhaps, she propped herself up with a metal walker. If there were a sweeter face anywhere in Tula Springs, Burma had yet to see it. The woman's fleshy arms quivered as she yanked herself a step closer to the cash register. Panting, she said, "My gran'chile, she on the *Ronald Reagan*."

"Pardon?" Leaning over the counter to hear better, Burma could see the slits in the sides of the woman's canvas shoes. Her soles burgeoned pink.

"She shippin' on that big boat they got."

Burma's eyes glazed over. Yes, she remembered the clip from TV years ago, Nancy Reagan smashing a bottle of champagne against the prow of the aircraft carrier. What could be more blasphemous than a Cancer draped in Dior christening a beast of Armageddon, a fire-breathing dragon that mortgaged the future of every child left behind? Was it any wonder that Burma refused to add a sales tax for her African American customers?

"That will be ninety-eight cents."

The woman dug out a five-dollar bill from a fold in her turban. As Burma reached into her metallic mini Fendi chef bag for change, she tried hard not to say, "I realize that your granddaughter probably wants peace in the world as much as I do, Ma'am," but out it came anyway. "And I deeply respect the sacrifice she's making for the lawmakers who aren't able to haul their fat asses down to Caracas and fight for the rigs themselves. But to rely on violence to bring about peace, well, violence is only going to beget more violence. With our tax dollars we allow the military to teach exactly what is forbidden by Jesus. Are you saved, Ma'am? Do you believe in turning the other cheek? Matthew five, forty-four: 'Love your enemies . . . do good to them that hate you.' This was Martin Luther King, Ma'am. He never lifted a finger against the racists who terrorized his—Ma'am? Don't go. Your change."

With one hand gripping the walker, which was aimed toward the exit, the woman stretched the other out behind her, as if she were afraid to look Burma in the face. Burma folded the change into the sweaty palm.

"You really hadn't ought to lecture people like that," Mr. Pickens remarked as the woman clumped the walker toward the door. "They got enough trouble as it is."

"You still here? Well, then, make yourself useful. Go help her out that door."

"I can't. You know Mrs. Pickens might . . ."

"Go!"

As he held the door for the customer, Burma snapped her Fendi bag shut. "Lord help me," she muttered, catching a glimpse of him hiding behind the woman's bulk as he edged sideways toward city hall.

BurgerMat, Redds's parent company, was doing a special nation-wide promotion. With a ShaqSiz coupon you could buy a *Snow White* DVD for $4.99. The dwarfs spoke Mandarin, which was why it was such a bargain. You had to read subtitles whenever they sang. Burma made sure the shopper who came to the register with twenty of the DVDs understood this.

"I swear, Carl Robert Pickens, what are you doing back here?" Burma demanded as the shopper, a svelte blonde who had wanted the DVDs for her daughters' soccer team, barreled away in her Expedition. The Mandarin hadn't discouraged this woman. Neither had Burma's sermon about what BurgerMat was doing to the rain forests. What was left, then, but to refuse to serve this gas-guzzling bitch since she was technically shoeless in very skimpy sandals? A sign plain as day announced NO SHOES NO SHIRT NO SERVICE. And who gave a flying fart if they were Manolo Blahnik sandals!

With a faint smile, Mr. Pickens held out his hand. There lay five crumpled hundred-dollar bills, which he quickly withdrew.

"She must have got into the till while we were having tea, Burma—the lady with that walker. I just knew this was going to happen someday. Now I don't want to hear another word. We're going to install our Code Orange Special this very afternoon."

Mr. Pickens moonlighted as an agent for a private security force. It was the only way he could afford a Miata with a superintendent's salary.

"You'll not only get a twenty-four-hour digital path to our home-land office, but we'll post a bonded guard on the premises."

Burma let him have his say, going into dollars and cents, before she reached into the vest pocket of his shot-silk jacket and yanked out the cash.

"The only thief on the premises is you, Mister."

"That's evidence, Burma. Give me back the evidence. I'll need it to get her booked. See, on the way out, I saw her stash it in that thing on her head, the turban."

"Bobby, that was *her* money. I gave it to her myself from my own chef bag."

"Your what?"

"My purse. And if you don't give it back to her this instant, I'll have you hauled into court, so help me Jesus."

Slack-jawed, with tendrils of sweat glistening on his pate, Mr. Pickens seemed as rooted as a pale gourd.

"Five hundred dollars? You just handed her five hundred in cash? Why?"

" 'Cause I felt like it, that's why. Now where is she? You better get your ass in gear, boy."

## A Stroll About the Grounds

Graceland II still needed landscaping. Mrs. LaSteele had convinced her daughter that this would help sell the house, some shapely trees and bushes to soften the raw look of Mr. Van Buren's bricks. The landscape architect had cancelled two appointments at the last minute before showing up forty minutes late for this one. Surely most multimillionaires didn't get treated this way. Burma felt like giving this man a good piece of her mind. Just

15

because she had on a Redds uniform, that was no reason for him to act so snooty.

"Estimate?"

"Yes, I'd like an estimate. How much to get those junipers you mentioned?"

Burma pulled down a white anklet to scratch. Chiggers abounded on the property, especially where she was now, in the saw grass that edged the biggest catfish pond. Dr. Schine, the landscaper her mother had selected for her, didn't seem affected at all, though. During their stroll through the grounds, he never bent over to scratch.

"Seventy, eighty."

"What?" Burma waved away a dragonfly that was buzzing her. "Seven thousand?"

"Seventy or eighty thousand, Mrs. Van Buren. Of course, that's without those fountains I mentioned. They'd run you another thirty— if I could get the marble I want."

"God a'mighty, I just thought some azaleas and . . ."

"Look, you want azaleas, you don't need me. Those junipers I mentioned are a rare ball variety that no one else in Louisiana has."

Though the sun wasn't visible behind a smoglike haze, Burma's eyes watered.

"Here," he said, unsnapping his attaché case.

The paper he handed her felt as bizarre as a fur teacup. After she dabbed her eyes, she realized it was a T-shirt.

"CEGAR? What's that supposed to mean, Dr. Schine? And what's this thing?"

A shrimp or an eel wove itself around the initials.

"Center for the Elimination of Growth Hormone Research," he said.

In a nearby stand of yellow pines, cicadas swelled to a fever pitch.

She found it hard to attend to his explanation—and broke in before he was finished.

"What's this got to do with landscaping? I just want a few trees put in."

"You could have the landscaping at cost, Mrs. Van Buren. Just let CEGAR use the premises and . . ."

"Why does it have an A in it? Hormone begins with H, doesn't it?"

Dr. Schine took her by the elbow and escorted her away from the pond. "As I was saying, children who are not average height are often treated with growth hormones. We find this practice disturbing."

"But you're a landscaper. What business is it of yours?"

"It's everyone's business, Mrs. Van Buren. Have you not noticed how large children are getting these days? It's not uncommon to see teenage girls six feet tall. Basketball players from China are now seven feet and over."

His touch, the very lightest, had a soothing effect. In the shade of a listing pine, she stopped squinting. "Well, it's good for girls to be big."

"Indeed? Did it ever occur to you what effect this has on the earth's resources? The calories a six-foot female must consume to maintain normal health as opposed to a four foot? Multiply this by four billion and you have some idea why our resources must be protected. CEGAR has calculated that a loss of five centimeters per year in the average height of the population of Louisiana could save two thousand acres of rain forest per annum."

"Really?"

"Every night millions of children go to bed hungry. Does this not concern you?"

"Of course it does. I worry about it all the time."

This indeed was the reason Burma hadn't given a dime to the Greater Tula Springs Arts Council. They wanted to name a building after her, but Burma could not in all good conscience let her money support rich snobs' framed magnolia blossoms when children were starving in Africa and when these same elitists awarded a blue ribbon to her mama's collage of Miss Brown. Yes, her mama snips out a picture of a shih tzu from a *Ladies' Home Journal* in her dentist's office, glues on an old head shot of her, Burma, in cap and gown, and wins first prize. *Excuse me?* You heard me, girl. First for a Phi Beta dog.

"Dr. Schine, please," Burma whispered hoarsely. His light touch had begun to wander as they strolled through the grove. At first it was a wispy brush or two, like a trumpet vine's, against her bare arm. But now it was a distinct pat on her fanny—or was that just a sumac snapping back into place?

"Yes, Mrs. Van Buren?"

"I, uh . . . As a matter of fact, I was going to give a bundle to a missionary society in Africa, not white missionaries, but native Igbos, Episcopalians. Then this friend of mine told me how these Igbos denounced that gay bishop in New Hampshire and persecute women they think are witches and, you know, how could I . . ." An idle probing finger, hers, felt something gooey on her fanny. "Dr. Schine, did you . . . Is there something on my tushy?"

"Your what?" He raised his sunglasses and peered at her outthrust pelvis. "Sap, Mrs. Van Buren. You must have brushed against a pine."

Her relief as they resumed their stroll—he a respectable foot or two ahead, droning on about calories, height, and the ozone layer—soon shaded into disappointment. Was that it? Was he giving up so easily? She could see now that there was no ring on his finger. And he smelled so heavenly, yes, like bread rising while a juicy yard hen baked tender and crisp with a sprinkling of paprika.

Oh, she was so hungry, starving. Mr. Van Buren, for all his faults,

never let her go hungry. On his eighty-first birthday, they had both
gone all out with extra-crispy chicken-fried steak, Dom Perignon,
and bunny love. Three-and-a-half times she had been bunnied that
afternoon before she had finally dozed off. Horny as hell from his
double prescription, that man never seemed to get his fill. Sadly, ever
since becoming a widow, the only time she managed to get rear-
ended was when Mr. Pickens hydroplaned into her Corolla. Oh, if
only she weren't a Christian, then she wouldn't have to worry so
much about whether this bunnying was the same as going all the way.
Mr. Van Buren had told her in the chat room it was the same as pet-
ting, which every religion allowed before marriage. It wasn't the
same as actual sex.

"Vinegar and mayonnaise."

"Huh?" she said, stumbling over a cypress knee.

"You want to get that sap out, Mrs. Van Buren?"

Dr. Schine fingered the stain after he helped her up from the bed
of brown cypress needles where she had lost her balance, collapsing
on all fours like Scarlett O'Hara in her barren garden, vowing never
to go hungry again.

"Mix a tablespoon of Blue Plate mayonnaise in a half cup of
vinegar," he said. "Rub it in right here in a circular sweeping motion,
not too hard."

The circular sweeping motion he was making she really shouldn't
allow, especially since he wasn't her type at all. The trouble was, she
had been fixated on Mr. Pickens for too long. Plump, almost woman-
ish, Mr. Pickens's pale washed-up physique, topped by a bland, in-
distinct nose, was what got her juices flowing. Dr. Schine was just a
mite too lean and tall and chiseled for an instant turn-on. But maybe
she could learn to . . .

"Dr. Schine, Heloise did hint that mayonnaise mixed with cigar ash was good for removing stains from dining room tables, but I've never heard of it being used on . . . Oh, no, Dr. Schine, please don't, please . . ."

But even before her protests were done, he had already stopped demonstrating the circular motion on the sap stain.

## Strictly Business

"What's got into you, girl?" her mother griped.

Yes, just like that. No thanks for taking her cross trainers back to PayLess for a half size smaller. No thanks for picking up Miss Brown's worm pills. No thanks for nothing. And she was itching like mad from those chiggers, too.

"Don't start in on me, Mama. I got a lot on my mind."

Should she call Mr. Pickens at home? Burma was wondering. After all, she had a right to know if the woman in the turban had got her five hundred dollars back. The gall of that man, not even bothering to tell her one way or the other. Before leaving Redds for her appointment at Graceland, Burma had tried reaching Mr. Pickens at city hall, but only got a recorded announcement. "All agents in Streets, Parks, and Sewers are servicing other complaints. We appreciate your complaint. It is important to us. You are number forty-two, with an estimated wait time of five minutes and thirty-five seconds. If this is an emergency, do not contact Mrs. Pickens at WaistWatch. Press the pound sign and hang up."

"Well, if you ask me, it's rude, plain rude." A bobby pin in her mouth, Mrs. LaSteele peeled the Scotch tape from a curl adorning her forehead. "I ask you to look presentable, Daughter, and this is the thanks I get."

"You never asked me to look presentable."

"A young lady should always look presentable, just in case."

Mrs. LaSteele squinted as she doused her ringlets with a mist that sent a wayward June bug on a downward spiral. "One never knows when one might be receiving."

"I'm too tired for company. And Mama, you really shouldn't use Black Flag on your hair."

"It's Final Net, Smarty-pants. Nonaerosol."

Although a Republican, Mrs. LaSteele was very big on recycling. She was in the habit of filling old containers with new products so as to help the trickle-down effect of the tax cuts. Burma had long ago stopped trying to fathom her reasoning on this score.

Mrs. LaSteele adjusted a drooping cameo on the collar of her Chinese silk dress. She invested lavishly in a Chinese wardrobe not just to encourage capitalism in that bastion of godless communism, but also because the high collars hid the scar from her goiter operation.

"This is not company."

"You mean a date? Mama, I told you I don't want you going on that computer ever again for me. I'm through with men."

"Who said anything about you?" Mrs. LaSteele held out an arm as delicate as a child's. "My shawl, please. No, not the lace. The fringe."

As Burma collapsed onto her mother's heart-shaped bed, a dozen charm bracelets dangling from a stuffed parrot tingled like a wind chime.

"I'm too tired for games, Mama. Just tell me who's coming over."

"I have a business appointment, if you must know." Screwing a pearl into an earlobe, Mrs. LaSteele added, "The least you can do is take off that uniform. And for heaven's sake, stop that scratching. Young ladies never scratch."

Through a blur of weariness Burma couldn't help admiring how trim and shipshape her mother looked. Being immoderately compact did help lessen the toll eighty-six years had exacted. Why, her mother could easily pass for sixty, Burma supposed, especially with that jet-black hair.

"They're here," Mrs. LaSteele announced just before the doorbell rang. Her blue eyes, sharp as tacks, could penetrate walls like George Reeves's did before his series was canceled and he died. "Go let them in."

With a groan Burma rolled off the bed and slouched toward the kitchen. There was a phone there, a cordless that belted out a motif from Strauss's *Elektra* whenever it got lost. As soon as her mama left, Burma decided she'd give that man a call.

"I'm not your maid, Mama. And who are these people, anyway? Is it church stuff again? I already told you I don't want any Baptists filling out report cards in this house. I swear I'll call the tax assessor if y'all try to swing any more votes."

"Go ahead and call," Mrs. LaSteele said, as she picked her way in spike heels to the front door. "Dolcheezza will inform you that she mimeographs the report cards for us, free."

At first the company was just a scent to Burma, the most delicious odor wafting through the kitchen door. Then, drawn closer for a peek from behind the swinging door, she saw the material, a summer fabric that shimmered like ebbing waves on a moonstruck beach in Mississippi. The kitchen door peeped open another inch or two as the company bent to plant a kiss on the chopstick holding her mother's bug-free bun in place.

"You shouldn't have," Mrs. LaSteele said, taking a nosegay of pansies from the company's hands. "You're very bad, Hunter."

Goosebumps prickled Burma's arm, as if a movie star had invaded their territory. Yes, there is something monstrous about celebrities, more than a hint of Boris Karloff in every Arnold. But Burma's frisson of horror had another source. This company— singular, not plural—was her landscaper, the very man who had talked her into an initial order of fifty-seven thousand dollars for dwarf juniper and Zen pebbles. Yes, despite her better judgment, he had somehow persuaded her that his low-maintenance grass-free landscaping would pay for itself. First of all, she wouldn't have to shell out for Mr. Joe to mow the grounds every two weeks. Plus, she'd be saving the ozone layer from all those fossil fumes Mr. Joe emitted when he backfired in the decrepit riding mower. But the real savings would come when she wasn't sued for every cent she had by Mr. Joe, who was bound to have an accident one day on that slippery rise by the catfish pond.

"No, Hunter, Her Majesty is indisposed," Burma heard her mother say in a stage whisper. "It's that time of month, you know. Now come along, or we'll be late. No, no, we'll take my Escalade. It's got a plasma you can watch while you eat. Ever see *Snow White?* Well, you got a treat coming, Mister. I just landed me a brand new DVD, the most up-to-date version with all the cuts removed. Daughter never seen me snitch it, neither."

After the business associates left, Burma marched herself into her mother's bedroom. Her own bedroom was so small that she'd had to store her suitcase beneath her mother's heart-shaped bed. But to get to the wheeled American Tourister, she had to first yank out a toaster oven her late father had been meaning to fix.

Yes, she had had it. She wasn't going to stay another minute in this den of iniquity. Imagine, shoplifting from her own daughter's store. And then running off with the daughter's landscaper when the daughter was too pooped to lay down the law. Didn't anyone have any values anymore?

But as the wheels squeaked over a floor furnace grate, Burma already had second thoughts. Did she really want to move back to Graceland II, all alone there in the country, miles from any help?

For a few months after her husband's death, Burma had lived there by herself, hoping for a quick sale to some rich, sleazy fan. She had tried to get her mama to move out there with her, but Mrs. La-Steele would have none of it. No sir, she wasn't fixing to relocate that stuffed parrot of hers one inch from where it always perched, right on top of her Bible.

The suitcase snapped open on Burma's bed. Beneath a Redds uniform that had shrunk one whole size after only a couple of washings in cold water, she found the bottle. Yes, a little nip of vodka would help her decide. Was it worse living here or living there?

In the kitchen she reached for a jelly glass. Maybe if Mr. Pickens installed an alarm at Graceland, then her mind would be more at ease. Or were break-ins like lightning: Once you got zapped, you didn't have to worry about getting zapped again? In any case, she had to ask him about that five hundred dollars, didn't she? Sure thing, she had plenty of reasons to give him a ring at home. But she'd need to fortify herself first with a belt or two.

"The superintendent's residence. State your business."

Of course it would be *her.* That woman had answered the phone, *Mrs.* Pickens. Well, Burma was a taxpayer. She had every right to ask the superintendent a question about public safety. There was nothing wrong with that.

"Hello, who is this?" the woman urged. "Speak up."

"Does lightning ever, you know . . . ?" Burma began, but her courage failed. Hyperventilating, she hung up. Yes, her heart was thumping just as madly as the night of the break-in at Graceland.

# Why Someone So Rich Lives with Her Mama

*A* smell had disturbed her sleep in the master bedroom of her late husband's mansion. When she clapped the Tiffany lamp on, though, the odor of verbena seemed more like a sound. Was it just a possum prowling around the garbage cans? Or had something broken into the house?

A bare foot probed for the library ladder that helped her in and out of the canopied bed, massive enough to make her feel a mere child. For some reason it wasn't there, this rolling ladder. As she hauled herself over the edge, she clung to the LibecoLagae linen so she wouldn't drop with a thud to the floor. Then, in Michael Kors crocodile platform sandals and an antique French lace peignoir— gifts from the deceased—she tiptoed down the service stairway, her heart pounding ferociously.

The light she switched on in the kitchen canceled out the flashlight's beam. Mute horror flickered between them for a moment, the intruder's nail file still inserted into the breakfront's lock.

Finally, Burma managed to say, "I don't believe we've met."

The intruder tugged at the nylon stocking flattening his nose.

"If you'll allow me . . ." She turned the brass handle on the Canterbury breakfront. "It's not locked. You won't need that thing."

But the intruder kept the nail file aimed at Burma as he backed into the archway that led to the dining room.

Something was not right about the intruder's gait. Not really a limp, it was still uncertain, as if the slight, boyish figure were negotiating a high wire.

"Pardon," he said to the carved pineapple he accidentally dislodged from the dado. "Sorry," he added, setting it back in place.

"The good china is over there," Burma said, as the intruder continued to grope his way backward, away from the kitchen light. "Over in that cabinet. It's not locked, so you can put that nail file away."

"With all due respect, Ma'am, this is no nail file."

"Well, whatever, just stop pointing it at me. There's no guns in this house. I gave them all away to the First Baptists after my husband passed. By the way, you're not Catholic, are you?"

"That's kind of personal."

"Sorry, I just wanted to make sure."

"What's the matter with this stuff, anyway?" The intruder tapped a Vera Wang dinner plate he had extracted from the sideboard in the dining room. "Why you giving it away?"

"That Duchesse pattern, you know how you sort of get tired of it."

Yes, she was tired of it, tired of all the fancy names that padded her life like two hundred pounds of unliposuctioned fat. It messed up her entire system. She wasn't regular anymore, and her breathing was off. She no longer took an easy breath, a good deep breath. A vague flutter of anxiety made it hard to think straight.

Oh, how she longed for those days when she could bitch about her paycheck; $249.54 was never enough for all she wanted. She yearned for things like the scarf at J. C. Penney's she couldn't afford, the turquoise scarf that would look so nice if Mr. Pickens ever asked her out . . .

"*You* tired, lady? You don't know what tired is."

The intruder ignored the good china she had pointed out and began rummaging through a drawer. "I haven't slept in a good ten hours. First I had to fill out all them insurance forms for Mr. Fred.

Then he makes me Mop & Glo the kitchen before I can set out to work. On the way my vehicle gets an aneurysm."

"Really? I thought only people got them."

"No, Ma'am, vehicles can get them, too. It's a bubble on the tire. Doesn't look like much, but you let it go, it'll give you a blowout."

"What kind of vehicle do you have?"

"There you go again, getting personal."

Burma pulled her peignoir closer to her ample bosom. "I just meant there's a lot of tires going to waste in the garage. You might want to check out there to see if there's something you could use."

"Too late now, I already had a new one put on. But maybe Mr. Fred, he might could use one."

"Who's Mr. Fred?"

"He's this preacher who's real old and poor and mean, a Latter-Day Saint. I check up on him twice a week, make sure he's O.K., since he hasn't got a family."

"How sweet," Burma said, yawning away a vague image of a singing senator's horseface.

"It's part of my volunteer work. By the way, where you keep the silver?"

"My husband's in-laws, they got to it first, boy."

And the good china she was trying to foist on the intruder, this had been awarded to her late husband's third wife, who had called Burma trailer trash in court. Yes, the woman had the gall to insist that Burma pack up all this Vera Wang herself and ship it, fully insured! Well, it would teach that dried-up beanpole a good lesson if every single Duchesse cup, plate, and saucer got itself stolen.

"Isn't there nothing silver left, Ma'am? Like stuff you use for sugar?"

Burma yawned as she extracted a bowl from the sideboard. "This is Villeroy & Boch. Sugar will look real nice in it."

"No, I mean for cubes."

"Sugar cubes? Well, hon, you can put sugar cubes in there for Mr. Fred."

"No, she said silver, those things that can pick up cubes."

"I told you, the in-laws got the Buccellati. All they left me is stainless steel."

"Got anything from Kay's Fine Jewelry in the mall?"

Burma sank onto a velvet side chair to ponder this. "What do you mean by 'she,' hon? Is Mr. Fred funny that way?"

"No, Ma'am, this is someone else I do favors for, not Mr. Fred."

"Is she real old like him—and poor?"

"No, but something's wrong with her leg."

"Well, boy, I just wished you'd showed up last week. That's when they come and hauled off all my silverware. Like a horde of locusts, those in-laws. You care for a cookie?"

"I best be going, Ma'am."

Burma wobbled slightly on the crocodile platforms as she headed back into the kitchen. "Hold on a sec, dear. I want you to try some of these new Oreos they got. They're Paul Newman, and it all goes to charity."

But when she returned to the dining room, both hands bulging with cookies, he had already fled.


"The First Baptists?" Burma's attorney asked the morning after the break-in. Burma wanted to make sure it wasn't illegal to not report an intruder to the neighborhood watch. So there she was in her attorney's office, explaining all the things the intruder didn't take.

"Why did you give all your husband's guns to the First Baptists?"

"'Cause Mama said they need a new organ. The one they got now has an F-sharp above middle C stuck."

The attorney sighed. Although she was a good ten years younger than Burma, she would have made the perfect mother-in-law. No matter how hard Burma tried, she just couldn't seem to do anything that Donna Lee Keely approved of.

"Do yourself a favor, Burma. Don't give anything else away until we've talked it over. You have no idea what harm you might be doing. It's like that check you mailed to the food pantry."

One hundred thousand dollars, that was what Burma had tried to give the priest at the pantry. But when the attorney caught wind of this from Mr. Harper, Burma got herself an earful. Don't you realize how little of the money would actually go to feeding the poor in Tula Springs? Donna Lee had demanded. Hush money, that's what the Vatican would use it for. Once the priest turned the money over to his bishop, Lord knows there'd hardly be enough left for a can of peas. So Burma had agreed to put a stop order on the check.

Settling down onto the attorney's sofa, Burma said, "This time I did ask, Donna Lee. I asked the intruder if he was Catholic before I showed him the china."

"What china?"

"The Vera Wang Mr. Van Buren's third wife is making me pack up and ship, insured. Why should I have to do all that work for that lazy, lying priss?"

"Because you didn't listen to me, that's why. Girl, I told you not to go on *People's Court*."

Hard as it was to admit, Donna Lee had been right again. The TV judge had been so mean to her, actually told Burma to wipe that smirk off her face. And she hadn't been smirking at all. She'd been fixing to cry, that's what! Oh, that judge had had it in for her from the very beginning just because the plaintiff used a cane and took about an hour to come down the aisle.

"In any case," Donna Lee went on, "you could hire someone to pack that stuff up for you. Lord knows you're <u>rich enough.</u>"

Burma slapped the gift she had brought for the attorney, a decorator box of premoistened tissue that was on sale at Redds. "Stop calling me rich! Any minute another shyster could crawl out of the woodwork and sue me for every cent I got. No offense," she added, as the attorney's jaw muscles began to twitch, "but it's true. I'm a sitting duck for any Tom, Dick, or Harry who trips on those aspidistras Mama won't let me trim away from her sidewalk. And you know full well I still got the government after me for back taxes."

Burma's late husband had refused to pay taxes on an installment of his lottery fortune, which he claimed had already been taxed. And he had a point. Every dollar spent on a lottery ticket by the millions of Louisiana taxpayers was a dollar already taxed by the feds. Was it his fault that the check they'd sent him was a mistake, gross not net? Both the computer that had cut the check and the clerk who stuffed it in the envelope had a virus.

"Yes, Ma'am," Burma went on after handing Donna Lee the latest notice from the IRS, "and all I hear is how nice the Republicans are to the rich, all these so-called tax breaks. Lord, if that isn't the biggest bunch of baloney. I hate them so much, girl. They just won't leave a poor widow alone, will they?"

"Nonetheless," Donna Lee said, filing the notice in one of Burma's many folders, "you can't encourage people to steal. That's not right."

"That boy didn't steal nothing, not even a tire. I tried to help him out because he seemed sort of sweet, like a first offense. But he was so darn picky. All he wanted was a silver spoon or something for this crippled lady's sugar bowl."

"Pardon?"

"He volunteers to help old folks and all. I could tell he had a good heart underneath that nylon stocking. Anyway, even if he didn't, I knew I could take him. But the next thief might not be all skin and bones, so frail. I'm worried, Donna Lee. I don't think I can stay at Graceland by myself no more."

"Perhaps if you locked the doors at night."

"I do. Only last night I couldn't remember if I had or not and I was too tired to traipse all the way downstairs again. That house is so big, you know, and would you please stop shaking that thing?"

The attorney had picked up an oatmeal canister from her desk. A crude cartoon balloon, "Impeach Pickens!" was appended to William Penn's benign smile.

With the dour cheer of the Salvation Army, Donna Lee gave the canister another shake. "O.K., you want to help people with your money, right? Well, then, get to the real root of the problem. No more Velveeta at the food pantry. No more Vera Wang and tires. Help me fight the corruption and injustice that keep the poor people poor."

Burma slapped the canister away from her face. "The super-intendent isn't corrupt."

"Maybe not, dear. Pickens doesn't have the gumption or the brains to be. But he's part of a totally corrupt system. You realize, of course, how he got elected. The same way our delightful mayor stole the election from Mayor Tyde. She and her cronies keep incorporating those phony whitebread subdivisions into Tula Springs. And by the way, if you truly want to help minorities, you won't encourage them to steal. You're actually aiding and abetting, Burma."

"Who said he was a minority?"

"You said he was African American, didn't you?"

"No, Ma'am. I didn't."

Donna Lee rattled the change in the canister. "As I was saying, a few thousand bucks, girl, it's nothing to you. And it'd make such a difference. We could get an ad in the paper, maybe even a few spots on TV."

"What would Mr. Pickens do without a job?"

"Let the Baptists worry about that. They always take care of their own."

Burma gazed sadly at William Penn. "No, Donna Lee, it's not right. He's my friend."

"Friend? Does a friend go ahead and marry some creep after you got down on your hands and knees and begged him, yes, begged him, to marry you?"

"I never got down on my . . . I just suggested . . ."

"And he'd been seeing Maigrite for a few weeks, that's all. You'd known him for thirty-five years, girl, all those years at Sonny Boy when he was your boss."

"It's your fault, Donna Lee. I never should have listened to you. No man wants a woman proposing to him."

"Oh, no? Just how do you think Mrs. Maigrite Pickens got him to marry her?"

"It was Jesus. She prayed to Jesus. Everyone knows that."

"Indeed? I suppose it was Jesus who gave her the false alarm, too."

"She couldn't help it if she thought she was pregnant."

"Burma, dear child, if Pickens was dumb enough to think a fifty-five-year-old could get pregnant."

"He thought she was thirty-seven! That's what that dagburn woman told him."

"There's just no end of excuses you'll make for that man, is there?"

The attorney had to step aside as Burma yanked open the frosted-glass door to the office. A premoistened tissue that Burma had been making even moister drifted onto the linoleum as the door wheezed shut.

"I hope you're satisfied," Burma grumbled as she clomped down the stairs. "I just hope you're good and satisfied, Miss Keely. Because of you I'm ending up all alone. Just another old maid living with her mama."

## The Return of Mrs. LaSteele

*W*hen she heard the key in the front door, Burma brushed a Saltine crumb off the muumuu she had changed into. She had a good mind to fling open that door and confront them both, catching Dr. Schine unaware as he helped her mother inside. *Just what the hell is going on, I'd like to know!* But she simply couldn't let Dr. Schine see her hair. It needed a wash and set.

"Still up?" Mrs. LaSteele said, as she tottered toward the refrigerator. A relentless First Baptist who went to church twice on Sundays, Mrs. LaSteele couldn't have been drinking. Burma simply refused to believe it. Yet there she was, steadying herself on the fridge door.

"Do you realize what time it is, Mama? I've been worried sick."

"It's eight-thirty." The fridge's pink light blinked on. "Now where's my prune juice, Miss? Did you drink it all again?"

Burma had, almost all, with the help of the vodka.

"You ought to be ashamed of yourself, Mama. Accepting pansies from a man half your age. And a man who just happens to be my landscaper."

33

Mrs. LaSteele's MedicAlert, custom-made to suggest her late Chihuahua, dangled into her daughter's cocktail. Burma shoved the tumbler aside to thwart her mother's sniffs.

"I'm fixing to test this, Burma. Give your mother a sip."

"No. You drink this and you'll hog the bathroom all night. I'll give you your juice in the morning."

A dreamy smile blurred Mrs. LaSteele's pert nose. Never had Burma seen such an expression on the normally anxious face, prepared at all times for the very worst.

"O.K., have it your way, Miss Boss of the World. I'll get out of your precious space."

Mrs. LaSteele banked out of the kitchen, Burma just behind. But her mother didn't make it to the bedroom. Instead she swooped down for an emergency landing on the bench of the Hammond organ.

"Just what have you been up to, Mama?" A hand to her mother's forehead told her there was no fever. In fact, she was strangely cool.

A few sharps blared as Mrs. LaSteele propped an elbow against the keys. Burma tried to flip off the power button but the red light stayed on. "Get off them black notes, Mama! I can't stand them black notes!"

"You been drinking, haven't you, daughter?"

"Me? Mama, you better tell me this minute where you been, or so help me I'm going out to your vehicle and print out the black box."

With a slight twitch the smile on her mother's face got even more smug. "Go right ahead. Track me down to the church annex."

"What? Y'all was at First Baptist?"

Mrs. LaSteele nodded.

"But Dr. Schine's a landscape architect."

"St. Paul made tents for a living. Dr. Schine makes gardens."

"I don't understand. Do you mean he's preaching to short folks?"

The logo on the T-shirt he had given her, the shrimp, came to mind. But all that stuff Dr. Schine had told her about the ozone layer and rain forests, it was science, not religion.

"Who you calling short?" A more familiar look flared in her mother's crystal-blue eyes. "For your information, I just happen to be normal, exactly what the normal person is going to look like in another three-and-a-half generations. That is, if we stop messing with those godless growth hormones."

Mrs. LaSteele plucked a lemon drop from a dish of hard candy.

"You and your daddy, all the cracks you used to make about me—"

"Mama, I never. That was Daddy done that."

"Oh, but you loved it, girl. Don't tell me you didn't eat it right up. I'm just sorry that man's not around to learn how abnormal he really was. Folks like him, they're going to be wiped right off the face of the earth. Along with their Beelzebubs, those evil SUVs."

"That doesn't sound very Christian, Mama—except for the last part. And I hate to remind you that you got yourself one of the biggest Beelzebubs they make."

Mrs. LaSteele's hand waved away an imaginary pest. "Thanks to *your* late husband. He's the one give it to me. I never wanted nothing that big. As a matter of fact, Dr. Schine is going to take care of it for me."

"What?"

Her mother's shapely legs, which didn't reach the floor from the bench, fluttered like a child's. With a sinking feeling, Burma glanced out the window.

Her mother always kept the curtains open day and night so that the neighbors could see that nothing untoward was going on inside *her* house. No, Mrs. LaSteele had nothing to hide, not a thing. And through these open windows, Mrs. LaSteele could also make sure that no one was tampering with her Escalade, which was usually parked on the lawn so that Burma's '84 Corolla could get out of the drive in the morning.

But now the eyesore beneath the street lamp wasn't there. Hurrying to the front window for a closer look, Burma saw only the ruts in the St. Augustine grass.

"Yes, he's got it, Burma. Dr. Schine is going to redeem it for me."

"Redeem it?"

"Don't worry that pretty head tonight. It's all taken care of. Now, if you don't mind, I'm going into my bedroom to see how *Snow White* turns out."


## The Five Hundred


*M*ore than once a customer at Redds might wander upstairs thinking there was a second floor of merchandise. But the attorney's office had nothing to do with Redds. Donna Lee Keely rented this former efficiency apartment not just because it was cheaper than the office-park leases that had sprouted up on the outskirts of town, but also because it was within walking distance for many of her pro bono clients.

When the superintendent of Streets, Parks, and Sewers rapped on her open door, he was too winded to talk. Those stairs leading up from the vestibule were so steep. Surely they were violating some sort of building code. Donna Lee herself, though she had recently backpacked two hundred miles along the Appalachian Trail to protest the Senate confirmation of yet another corporate polluter as head of the EPA, would often halt midway to catch her breath.

*Do you have an appointment, Pickens?* she almost asked. But the ashen look on the man's face alarmed her. Taking him by the elbow, she steered him to a worn sofa near the drone of a window unit. With a nod, he accepted the paper cup of water from the cooler.

"O.K.?"

His mouth agape, he idly fingered her wilting African-mask plant.

"My leaves," she admonished as his panting subsided. "Please don't. They're sensitive."

Twenty years ago this man had been her secretary, back when she had worked for Mr. Herbert's firm. After Donna Lee had sued Mr. Herbert for not making her a partner (she lost the sex discrimination suit thanks to a judge who had installed a half-ton bust of Mel Gibson in the courthouse foyer) Mr. Pickens had wanted to follow her into private practice. This, of course, was out of the question. Though he had some ability when it came to filing, Mr. Pickens, like the Old South, conveyed an aura of defeat. His very presence sapped her energy for vigorous reform and justice for all.

"This turban . . . ," he finally managed to say.

The cooler bubbled as she refilled his cup. "What turban?"

"There's this lady—thanks." In one gulp he emptied the cup. "She had on this turban, and I caught her stealing the other day, see, only now Burma's claiming she gave her this money, and she's too scared to take it back."

"Burma is?"

"No, this heavyset lady who came into Redds." He gasped for air. "You really ought to invest in an elevator, Miss Keely. I've got a friend in city hall who could cut you a deal. An Otis might run you . . ."

"Mr. Pickens, as you can see, I'm very busy." She rattled the pages of a deposition for a divorce proceeding, her bread and butter. "I don't have time for any nonsense." The stapler banged down with admirable authority, though she had no idea what she was stapling. "How much is it, anyway?"

"The elevator?"

"The money she took."

While mopping his brow with a handkerchief he slipped the hundred-dollar bills from his vest pocket. "She had it tucked away in her turban."

They both regarded the five hundred dollars that he had placed on top of the deposition.

"Who is she? What's her name?"

Mr. Pickens shrugged as he put the bills back in his pocket. "Just some customer in there buying clothespins. Burma and I were in the back room, and she must have got her hand in the till, this lady."

"What were you and Burma doing in the back room, Mr. Pickens?"

"We were drinking—Uh, I mean, Mrs. Van Buren has some drainage problems and needs a cam down her pipe."

"What?"

"Her office has this sink, and the city's videocam for sewers, it's on the fritz, so I was telling her that—"

"Drinking?"

"Water, tap water. I was parched. Anyway, I think this lady lifted the money from the till, and then Mrs. Van Buren, you know how she is, she tried to cover for her. Said that she *gave* her the five hundred. Now if that lady had been white—and a man—I bet Burma would've—"

"Dammit." Donna Lee swatted the hand that had strayed back to her potted plant. For a brief moment outrage revealed a hint of character in the superintendent's face.

"I'm sorry, Pickens. But I wish you'd just keep your hands to yourself."

Of course, this was a displaced swat, which made Donna Lee feel a little guilty. She had just glimpsed another spot on her hand. Age spots? Yet she was barely fifty. And didn't she read somewhere that fifty today is what thirty used to be?

"It's high time that girl woke up and smelled the coffee," Donna Lee said, tossing the hand lotion that promised miracles into her desk drawer. It slammed shut with such force that Mr. Pickens's mouth unhinged.

"What?"

"Nothing," he said. "I mean, I agree."

"Think of all the good that money could be doing. Millions she's got, enough to shake this town up good. And what does she do but try to give it away to petty thieves and Catholics. What?"

He cleared his throat again. "Maybe if you encouraged her, Miss Keely. She's got such a wonderful opportunity now with Graceland and all. The IMAX."

"What IMAX?"

"Didn't Burma mention it to you? You know all the problems she's been having with the IRS. Well, her accountant says this will square her with them—and then some. She'll never have to worry about taxes for the rest of her life."

Donna Lee ignored the phone ringing and sat down. "Mr. Harper? Is that who you're talking about?"

She glanced at the caller ID again: Yes, it was Mary Jo Harper, someone she'd rather not talk to in front of Mr. Pickens. Mary Jo, her client, was in the process of divorcing Mr. Harper, and some very personal financial matters were being negotiated.

"Aren't you going to get that?" Mr. Pickens asked.

Donna Lee glared at him. "Just what do you mean by an IMAX? How will that help her tax situation?"

"It's educational. Burma will be enlightening thousands of

schoolchildren every year at Graceland. See, it's historic, that property. Without it, we might all be in Cuba now, speaking Spanish."

"Huh? What *are* you doing?"

While talking, Mr. Pickens had begun removing some contraption from a brown bag he had lugged into the office.

"You should always test an appliance before bringing it home," he said, unplugging her lamp so that he could plug in his own cord.

"What the hell is that?"

"A Presto TacoMaker. They're on sale now at WalMark."

"Wonderful. I'll rush right down."

"You might get yourself an answering machine while you're at it," he said.

Donna Lee, of course, didn't believe in answering machines. Either you were there or you weren't. Period.

"Careful!" she said as Mr. Pickens backed his taco maker into the oatmeal canister on her desk. "Leave it, just leave it."

But he went ahead and scooped up the change that had fallen out of the canister onto the linoleum.

"Keely here," she barked into the phone, which just wouldn't stop ringing. Why did that woman keep ringing when it was obvious no one was there? "Hold a sec, Mary Jo. Pickens, I said *leave* it."

The change clattered back into the canister as the taco maker's cord got tangled in his tie. Choking a little, he didn't seem to notice what the Quaker was saying on the oatmeal canister. Neither did Donna Lee get a chance to ask him what the hell he meant about Cuba. Her client on the other end of the line was feeding her a steady stream of invective about Mr. Harper.

As the superintendent backed out the frosted-glass door with his Presto, he pretended not to hear Donna Lee's command to wait outside until she got off the phone. After all, she wasn't his boss anymore.

# Chez Pickens

"You did what?" he demanded.

At the sink Mrs. Pickens went on scrubbing the burnt dough off the Presto TacoMaker's detachable rollette. "Presto, my ass bucket. You bring home another time-saver like this, Superintendent, you're going to get a presto right upside your head."

Mr. Pickens gazed at the charred cornmeal on his plate. She had told him he wasn't to get up from the table till he finished every last bite. Well, we'll see about that, he thought, almost rising from the dinette chair.

"I'm not sure I heard right, Mrs. P. Did you just say you found five hundred in my vest pocket and—"

"You heard me."

"And what? What did you do with it, dear? That's not my money. It happens to belong to—"

"I know darn well who it belongs to, Mr. Pickens. And I'd thank you not to talk with your mouth full."

He swallowed dutifully, then coughed as a crisp edge of a taco scraped the wrong pipe going down. Gagging, he reached for the glass she held out from the sink.

"Thanks," he muttered after emptying the glass.

"Thanks yourself. Another glass to wash."

"I told you I'd do the dishes."

She gave her chiffon apron, which she had just untied, a vigorous snap, virtually in his face. "What kind of man does dishes, tell me that?"

As she wrapped a fresh organza apron around her wasp-thin waist, he ventured, "Clint Eastwood did, in *Hang 'Em High*. Anyway, why don't you let those things soak? It's our anniversary, after all."

"Some anniversary. Me, I get a taco maker when he knows I can't stand shredded lettuce. Him, he gets an engraved two-hundred-dollar tie clip."

Mr. Pickens fingered the gold heart pierced by a zircon-studded arrow. "Two hundred for this? You got to be kidding. Just how much is Brother Moody paying you?"

Even though they were married, Mrs. Pickens kept her finances completely separate. She had her own checking and savings accounts and never revealed the balances, much less her WaistWatch salary.

"What makes you so nosy? I never knowed a man so nosy in my entire life. Next thing you know, you'll be asking for my birth certificate."

Her back still to him, he mused again over the uncanny resemblance. It was almost as if Toinette herself were at the sink. Both Mrs. Pickens and her niece, Toinette Quaid, had the same amazing waist, which yielded to an oddly voluptuous rear end. Odd because both niece and aunt were so frail looking, almost anorexic. Whenever Mr. Pickens thought he couldn't stand another word from his wife, a mere glimpse of her from the rear made life possible again, ripe with a nostalgia for better days, when he was so young, head over heels in love with the candy clerk at Sonny Boy. Oh, Toinette, Toinette, to think that I was your boss back then, that we shared the same space eight hours a day, five days a week except for those wretched holidays, Columbus Day, Flag Day . . .

"You hear me?"

"What? Yes, yes."

"Then move it," Mrs. Pickens said. "March."

Relieved that he really didn't have to finish the charred tacos she had prepared, Mr. Pickens scraped the chair back and headed for the garbage can.

"What the tar you doing, Mr. Pickens? Put that trash bag down."

"I thought you wanted me to . . ."

"You don't listen, do you? You don't listen to a thing I say."

A single tear coursed down her cheek. In her hand-stitched apron she did indeed look as frail as her niece used to.

"I'm sorry, Mrs. P. What is it?"

"I asked you to go make Edwin stop barking. It's not good for my nerves."

"Yes, of course." The screen door swung open as Mr. Pickens went to deal with the neighbor's schnauzer.


Three hours later it was still light. Yet Mrs. Pickens was already on her knees beside her twin bed. "Give me understanding, Lord," she prayed aloud, both hands folded tight in front of her Kabuki face, masked by cold cream.

In his own bed, Mr. Pickens was absorbed by another recommended reading from Burma. Though he had enjoyed Molly Ivins, it didn't hold a candle to this one, Kitty Kelly on Babs Sumach's first term in office. Did you know that Babs had been a go-go dancer during the Vietnam War? That she had had both her name (Schumacherzen) and breasts reduced? Of course, the book had to be disguised. Mr. Pickens had slipped the cover of *Treason* over Kitty's jacket.

"Thank you, dear Lord, for sending me this cross I must bear day after freaking day. I know that everything you send must be good for me, helping me develop patience and fortitude. Stop chewing."

"I'm not chewing," the cross muttered, turning a page.

"You're making that chewing noise again."

With a manicured nail Mrs. Pickens activated a scent dispenser plugged into the outlet by her bed.

"Thank you also for the five hundred dollars that help make up for the anniversary gift he gave me. You, at least, had the good sense to know, dear Lord, that I'm worth more than a taco maker."

"That money didn't come from Jesus, dear. You're going to have to give it back."

Another hiss as a kiwi-fig odor blanketed the room.

"Bless Aunt Hanks and Dewey, and remember cousin Gin-Gin is the one who hates chimpanzees, so let her win the school board election. Good night. Oh, and if you see Lou Jones up there, please forgive her for the way she used to be down here on earth, always trying to stir up trouble between me and my lawfully wedded husband, telling me when she came back from lunch that she'd seen Mr. Pickens over at Redds, and now the new assistant I got down at WaistWatch, she's telling me he goes in the back door of Redds every day at four P.M., just like clockwork, and it's my anniversary today, and if You don't think I have a right to that five hundred dollars that hussy at Redds gave him, the one who calls here drunk and hangs up when he doesn't pick up, then You tell me right now. Go ahead. I'm waiting."

Mr. Pickens's mouth opened. Then shut.

"Good. Now that's settled. Amen."

# A Campaign Contribution

*M*r. Harper was zipping up his trousers when the door, which Donna Lee thought was locked, wheezed open. Instinctively, she gave the accountant a little shove, as if to propel him toward some exit. But the only exit was the frosted-glass door Mr. Pickens was now leaning against, panting.

"Well, well," Mr. Harper said, with a somewhat bland, menacing smile, "if it isn't my favorite assessor. Miss Keely, I'd like you to meet Fred Pickens, our illustrious tax assessor."

Since Mr. Harper was holding out his hand, Mr. Pickens shook it. "Actually," he said, "I'm not the assessor. I'm the commissioner of parks and stuff."

Donna Lee sighed. There was nothing quite like being in a roomful of Republicans. "Actually, Mr. Harper, his name is Bobby, not Fred. And he's the *superintendent* of Streets, Parks, and Sewers."

Mr. Pickens cleared his throat. "Garbage. It's Garbage now."

"How 'bout them Otters!" Mr. Harper clapped Mr. Pickens on the shoulder with one hand while tucking in his shirt with the other. "Go, Otters!"

Filling a cup at the water cooler, Mr. Pickens said, "They got football at St. Jude again? I thought it was over since the termites got into the stadium, the Formosas."

When he turned around, though, he found he was talking to thin air. Neither Mr. Harper nor Donna Lee was in the room.

. . .

She was back in a moment or two. "What is it, Pickens? I'm extremely busy this morning."

"It's about that five hundred dollars. See, my wife found it in the vest pocket of my Armani last night and—What was Mr. Harper doing here?"

Donna Lee's eyes strayed to the sofa cushion, a few inches from where Mr. Pickens had plopped down. That was where the condom lay, pale and shriveled.

"Armani, Mr. Pickens? How nice. I'm glad our city employees can afford designer clothes."

"It's his K–Mart line, thank you very much. So what was Burma's accountant doing here, Miss Keely? Did he violate one of your sumptuary laws?"

"Mr. Harper happens to be a client of mine," Donna Lee said, pounding her stapler. "Someone I'm suing."

"You're suing a client?"

"My client, Mary Jo Harper, is suing Travis—Mr. Harper—for divorce, Mr. Pickens. Do you want me to draw you a diaphragm? Now what did you barge in here for? Did it ever occur to you to knock?"

"That sign downstairs, 'Walk-Ins Welcome,' is that a lie?"

While he leaned over to refill his cup from the water cooler, Donna Lee snatched the condom and tossed it in the clay pot that held the African mask. The wastebasket was already filled to the brim.

"Anyways," he went on, "this is an emergency. I got to get that five hundred back from Mrs. Pickens or Burma will raise a stink."

He leaned forward, squinting at the attorney as if she were far away.

"What's the matter, Pickens?"

"You got something in your hair, I think."

"I think it's none of your business."

He shrugged. "Anyways, I don't have enough ready funds to cover the whole five hundred myself. All I could round up for now is sixty dollars, sort of a down payment. So here."

As he struggled to remove an ungainly wallet from his trousers, Donna Lee, after a brisk pat down, dislodged a Trident wrapper from her hair. Odd how every time she insisted on not making out with Travis during office hours, she'd wind up with a gum wrapper somewhere on her person. And he had sworn not to chew around her anymore.

"It's not safe in my house," Mr. Pickens said, handing over the twenties. "I can't keep any cash around now, Miss Keely, not since our anniversary. And I don't want Burma to see how much is missing, so if you don't mind holding onto this for now."

Donna Lee put one of the twenties he had handed her up to the lamplight. "Good a place as any, Pickens, till we get this whole thing resolved. Burma simply can't go on letting thieves off the hook. Someone's got to talk some sense into her."

"Can I get a receipt, Miss Keely?"

"No. Not till you cough up the rest, four hundred forty. And by the way, why don't you just tell your wife she's taken stolen money, evidence for a trial?"

"You think I haven't tried? Whenever I try to explain that five hundred was filched from the cash register at Redds, Mrs. Pickens wants to know what I was doing over there in the first place. I try to explain about Burma's pipe that needs plugging, only the cam is—"

"Please stop that!"

"What?"

"I've asked you time and again, Pickens, not to fiddle with my leaves."

He glanced at the African mask leaf between his fingers. "Sorry.

So it's like I can't convince her that Burma didn't give me the money herself. Mrs. Pickens is the suspicious type, you know."

"By the way, since you're so chummy with Burma, why don't you get her to agree to that IMAX?"

On the sofa a few minutes earlier, Donna Lee had managed to probe Travis—Mr. Harper—about this scheme for Graceland. Coming up for air, he had explained all the tax benefits involved. What he didn't have time to explain, though—thanks to Mr. Pickens's entrance—was why he hadn't bothered to mention this to her before.

"I'm not anyone's chum, Miss Keely. I'm married."

"If Burma doesn't donate Graceland to AmStar, it's likely the IRS will attach it. Tell her that."

"Tell her yourself."

"I can't. She's not speaking to me. Hangs up every time I call, Pickens. We had another fight."

He was staring at her funny again, a little cockeyed. "Well, you know how Burma is about war. She never looks on the bright side, like how that war kept us from having to learn the subjunctive. That's the only F I got, in Spanish II with Miss Pottle. Remember her?"

"The IMAX, Pickens. We're talking about the IMAX."

"I know, that's what Burma told the lady with the turban, how her granddaughter hadn't ought to be on the *Ronald Reagan* when she was looking for parakeet seed."

Donna Lee couldn't bear another minute of his nonsense. The way he was looking at her, as if *she* had a screw loose, well, it was too weird. Firmly, yet civilly, she ushered him out the door before he could finish explaining about the aircraft carrier's shortage of clothespins.

As the superintendent headed downstairs, Donna Lee pondered the IMPEACH PICKENS oatmeal canister. Sixty bucks couldn't hurt.

And it would serve that man right for not marrying Burma. But no, she really couldn't.

Bending down for a manila envelope in her bottom desk drawer, Donna Lee noticed for the first time her blouse. Travis—Mr. Harper—had unbuttoned it, dangerously low. And all that time Mr. Pickens hadn't said a word about it! Just sat and gawked.

Two buttons, three were rebuttoned, then four, up to the primmest schoolmarm top. After that, with no qualms at all, she stuffed the sixty bucks into the Quaker Oats. Thinking more clearly now, she realized that she'd never prosecute any woman in a turban for redistributing a few bucks from Redds. After all, wasn't Redds part of that ghastly corporation that was turning rain forests in Brazil into Whoppers? Let the money go for something worthwhile.

## Human Resources

*A*ccording to the bylaws of BurgerMatCO, of which Redds was a wholly owned subsidiary, the assistant manager of any Class D franchise was, *Deus vult*, chair of human resources. Burma took this aspect of her job seriously. Her interviews for the current vacancy, manager, had so far been futile. Almost everyone who had applied for the job turned out to be either a friend or relative of her mother's. And let me tell you something, Burma Van Buren was not about to have a puppet regime installed at Redds, no sir. She got enough bossing around at home.

This was why Burma started the thirty-ninth interview in the assistant manager's office with: "Are you or have you ever been consanguine with an employee of this company or parent corporation, which includes any relation, legal or otherwise, to Mrs. Gyrene Hattie LaSteele or worshipped in any capacity at the First Baptist over on Board Street?" Of course, this wasn't written into the official questionnaire BurgerMatCO made her read aloud. This was a rider Burma pretended to read.

"No," the candidate replied.

"Be seated."

Dr. Schine nudged the aluminum lawn chair a little closer to the desk while Burma, still not looking him full in the face, rubber-stamped a pile of invoices with remarkable bureaucratic zeal.

"Dr. Schine," she said after a final good whack, "I'm not going to mess around the bush with you. I'm a straight shooter, tacky as that might seem to some folks. So let me lay it out for you: I don't plan on hiring a perjurer for manager of this establishment."

"Indeed?"

"You just declared that you have no relation with Mrs. Gyrene LaSteele."

"No blood relation."

"But you do have an *otherwise* relationship, I'm afraid. Furthermore, you *have* worshipped at First Baptist on Board Street."

"We were actually at the annex on the corner of Myrtle. And I worshipped no one. I simply gave a scientific presentation to some of the more diminutive members of the congregation."

His yawn was accompanied by such a voluptuous stretch that his legs rose clear off the linoleum. Yes, the soles of his shoes (clean enough to eat off, she couldn't help noticing) were looking her square in the face. Burma had read somewhere that in the Sahara desert, this was about the rudest thing you could do, show someone your soles. But she herself was too well brought up to mention it.

"Look, before I accept this position here, Mrs. Van Buren, I'd like to get one or two things straight. First of all, I'm not sure I like the idea of having an employee of mine, someone I might have to discipline on occasion, going around with a swell head just because she's worth a hundred million or so."

Burma's eyes blazed. "That's a lie, a damn lie! Who told you that? It's barely thirty-six, and at the rate I'm being taken to the cleaners, five lawyers suing me now and the government hounding me for taxes my husband didn't pay—my *late* husband, that is, poor dear, very dead now—thanks."

She blew into the handkerchief he'd tossed onto the toe of one of his buttery-soft shoes.

"Everyone thinks it's so easy being rich," she said after a hiccup or two. "They haven't a clue. It just saps you, Dr. Schine, drains the life plum out of you. It's a full-time job being rich, period, believe me. But just try being rich *and* Christian, see how you like them apples. Jesus says if a thief asks for your shirt, give him your cloak. So I try to give this burglar all my good china, and he won't be satisfied with nothing but the silver I already had snatched out from under me by my in-laws. Then I try to help this poor customer that come in the other day, give her cash she won't have to report to the IRS, and what happens? Some big shot from city hall swipes the money from that poor lady and won't even call me about it."

"Hm."

"That's right, all my money seems to end up helping the greedy. Like one minute you got a vehicle setting in your front yard, the next, it's gone."

"Redeemed."

He nudged the sleeve of her uniform with one of his miraculously clean soles. How was it possible that she wasn't telling him to get his big ugly feet—*wow, those boys were something else!*—off her

51

desk? Why, if Mr. Pickens ever tried anything like this, she'd have knocked him clear into Sunday week.

"I thought you hated SUVs, Mrs. Van Buren."

"I do."

"So what's your problem? You got rid of an eyesore, that's all, something cluttering up your yard. You should be thanking me. And besides, it's not your vehicle. If I'm not mistaken, your late husband transferred the title to your mother after he bought a Hummer."

"Go ahead, rob me blind. See what I care."

Was it paprika or cumin? Oh, that bittersweet aroma wafting from those heavenly soles . . .

"You ever get that stain out, Mrs. Van Buren?"

Burma glanced down at her uniform, which had been nudged again. "No. Your recipe didn't work."

"What kind of mayonnaise you use?"

"Blue Plate, just like you said. The nonfat kind."

For a man with such sharp chiseled features, he sure did have full lips, pouty as a female amnesiac's on a daytime soap.

"There you go: nonfat. You got to use the regular mayonnaise, Mrs. Van Buren, with all the lipids left in."

"Oh."

"You get that stain out, I'll show you how to give." The soles tapped together mildly. "Really give."

Burma reddened. "Oh, Dr. Schine. I do *so* want to give. It's been so long, too. I think I might've forgot."

His heel alighted on an application form. "Where do I sign?"

# For a Good Cause

Squatting in front of the compact fridge a client had bartered for her services, Donna Lee searched for the hummus. She knew she had brought it to work that morning. The fridge shuddered as her hand probed behind something sticky the client, a fifty-year-old sophomore at St. Jude who had sued for an A, had left behind.

"*Eeek!*"

Something had brushed her collar.

It was only Burma, though, who had crept into the room and breathed down her neck.

"Can't anyone in this friggin' town knock!"

"The door was open."

"Lord, thought you were that mouse," Donna Lee said, trying to stand. Her knees ached something awful. And all she had done was squat for a minute.

"You don't happen to have any humane traps downstairs, Burma, do you?"

"Actually, I just come up to borrow one from you."

On the conference table behind a stack of depositions for the Harper divorce, Donna Lee spied the hummus. It made her feel better. She wasn't losing her mind, after all.

"Why don't you stay for Bible study, Burma?"

Burma had missed the last two meetings, mainly because she wasn't speaking to the group leader, Donna Lee. It was Pickens, of course, that was keeping them apart. Burma still refused to give a dime to the impeachment campaign. But Donna Lee wasn't about to give up. If it was the last thing she did, she'd put that woman's money to good use.

"I can't, Donna Lee. We're doing inventory."

"Oh, come off it." Donna Lee held out a glass of Shiraz. It was nice to be on speaking terms again, although the occasional hiatus was also refreshing. "Don't be such a priss. Take a swig."

"All you do is insult me, Donna Lee. Up one side and down the other. Did it ever occur to you I might have feelings?"

"God, yes. That's about all you have these days."

"There you go again!"

Burma gulped down half the wine in the Lalique crystal stemware she had given Donna Lee for her fiftieth birthday.

"I swear, Donna Lee, you're about the meanest, most inconsiderate . . ."

Thrusting a King James into Burma's free hand, Donna Lee ushered her to the Goodwill sofa. "You want a real friend in your life, girl, or some phony ass licker?"

"Give me the ass licker," Burma said from the depths of the sofa, where she had settled with the wine.

After studying her a moment, Donna Lee plucked a bar code off the assistant manager's Eton collar. "I'm serious. Just because you inherited a shitload of taxpayers' hard-earned money . . . It's criminal how the government cons poor people into thinking they have a chance at winning anything."

"For your information, I never once bought a lottery ticket, not once in my entire life. Say, this stuff is good."

Donna Lee topped her wine off before opening the book on Burma's lap. "We're doing Exodus tonight. Twenty-one."

"I told you I got inventory. Besides, I can't stand that Dutchboy woman."

"Grady? What you got against her?"

Burma took another healthy swig. "Her hair. She looks like that boy on the paint cans. And she makes me feel like a damn fool. Just because I believe in Jesus."

Donna Lee stuck her finger in the hummus for a sample. "Do you also believe in slavery? The Bible, of course, endorses slavery. Tonight it's showing how a man can sell his daughter into slavery."

"Neither Jew nor Greek, neither bond nor free—"

Donna Lee snatched the Bible and peered intently at 21. "Where do you see that?"

"Neither male nor female are we in Jesus."

"Hold your horses, girlie. We haven't got to Jesus yet. By the way, our supplemental text this week is *The Handmaid's Tale*."

"I thought we were doing Kitty Kelly."

"Burma, dear, that was ages ago."

"Wonderful. I shelled out thirty bucks for the hardback."

"Well, if you didn't keep missing meetings . . . Here." Donna Lee held a hunk of pita in front of Burma's nose, as if tempting an ungainly pet. "I hope by now you've been giving some thought to the impeachment."

"I sure have," Burma said, munching. "It's the most immoral thing I ever heard of."

"Stop being so judgmental."

"You're not getting one red cent from me."

"O.K., fine. But once Pickens gets impeached—and he will, whether you contribute or not—we're going to need someone to stick her thumb in the dike."

"Don't look at me. I'm into men."

"I'm serious. You'd be a great replacement."

"No, sir, Donna Lee, no way. I'm not getting involved in your feuds. If you're so hot and heavy about impeaching him, then why don't you step up to the plate yourself?"

"An atheist? I don't think so."

"You're no atheist, not a real one."

"Well, whatever God I believe in, it's not the one who stops the earth revolving so there's a little more time to slaughter women and children. No, Burma, we need a good, solid Christian for this campaign. Think of all the good you could do with your money. Why, once you've replaced Pickens as superintendent, you could saturate the media, unmask all the lies the corporate polluters—what's this?"

Donna Lee fingered a pale glob on Burma's uniform, then sniffed. "Mayonnaise! Oh, Burma, I thought we made a pact."

"I wasn't *eating,* I swear. I was just—"

"Don't lie to me, girl. I can see plain as day—oh, that must be Grady." A muffled voice called again from the stairwell. "Go in the closet there and get out the Bibles."

"I told you I can't stay."

"Sure you can. Hey, Gradation! Come on in, babe. You remember Burma from downstairs, don't you?"


After Grady Morgen left with the guest she had brought with her, a Kant specialist from St. Jude Community College, Donna Lee collected the wineglasses.

"You mind rinsing these out downstairs?"

Burma blew out a scented candle, sandalwood. "I'm not your maid. And I got all that inventory. By the way, do you realize how poor Kant specialists are?" She shook the IMPEACH PICKENS canister beside the candle. "Making her put in twenty bucks."

"I didn't make her. It was only a suggested donation. Oh, I've been meaning to tell you. Pickens came by this morning with sixty bucks. I hope you don't mind, but I'm keeping it there."

"Where? In this oatmeal?" Burma pried open the lid and fingered the bills inside the canister. "You got to be kidding."

"I'm just keeping it there for now. See, it's part of that five hundred."

"The money he stole from that lady, right? Where the hell is the rest I'd like to know?"

"Pickens never stole anything. You got the wrong thief."

"That lady in the turban never took a cent."

"Whatever. The problem now is that Pickens's wife, well, she took the money out of his Armani jacket and . . . Yes, may I help you?"

"Pardon," the man said with another tap on the open door. "By any chance is Mrs. Van Buren here?"

For the life of her Burma couldn't figure out why someone with a Ph.D. would say something that stupid. She was standing there plain as day.

"I'll be down in a minute," she said to the man. "Go on back to the store, hear. I'm busy."

"Lord," Donna Lee said, as the stairwell echoed with his footsteps, "who was that? Hunk City down there, girl."

"It's just the new manager I'm breaking in."

"You know, Burma, you do look tired. Let me go downstairs and rinse these glasses in your sink. You can straighten out the office for me here, put away the hummus."

"Never mind," Burma said, taking the tray of stemware from her. "What's his name?"

"I liked to die when Grady knocked over her glass tonight. You hadn't ought to use this Lalique around her, Donna Lee."

"His name, girl. What's your boss's name?"

"He's not my boss!"

That was the whole point, of course. Dr. Schine promised not to boss her around if she hired him as manager. As a matter of fact, he promised to let her be the real boss, even though she was officially known as assistant manager. And besides, if she *hadn't* hired him right away after turning down thirty-eight other candidates, the vice president of human resources in Little Rock was going to send a real manager who would make her life a living hell.

In any case, Dr. Schine hated BurgerMat as much as she did. Finally she had found someone who cared about the rain forests.

"He's the manager, yes," Burma replied when Donna Lee repeated this fact. "But it's a democracy down there. Everyone has equal weight."

"I see. So what's this equal weight's name?"

Burma had set the tray down on the conference table. She reached for a half-empty glass and took a gulp. "If you must know, it's Dr. Schine."

"Doctor?"

"Yes, Doctor. And if you don't mind, I think I'll take this sixty bucks."

Donna Lee yanked the oatmeal canister out of her friend's reach.

"It doesn't belong to you, Donna Lee."

"Well, it's not yours, either. You said it belongs to that woman in the turban. As soon as I see her, I'll—"

"You know who she is?"

"No. But—hey, did you say Schine?" Donna Lee spit an olive pit into the African mask to nourish the soil. "Is he related to your landscaper?"

"No."

The look Donna Lee aimed at Burma made Burma feel even worse. But what had she done wrong? Nothing. Nothing whatsoever.

"Burma LaSteele, that man *is* your landscaper, isn't he?"

She shrugged. "I've got to go finish up downstairs, show him the ropes."

"What's with this 'Doctor' business?"

"Ph.D.'s got to eat same as anyone else. He's got one in sociopathy."

Donna Lee blew out another candle. "Sociopathology? How does that qualify him to landscape your yard?"

"Doesn't take a rocket scientist to dump gravel all over the place. Besides, his dissertation was on lawns."

"The De-Maculation of Whiteness in Postcolonial Trailer Park Paradigms" would be closer to the truth. But Burma was already on her way out the door with the tray of crystal stemware. Honestly, some people were plain ignorant when it came to degrees, and how hard it was to find a decent tenure-track job.

## To the Rescue

*M*r. Pickens was trying to decipher the invoice for repairing the videocam for sewer inspections when she waltzed into his office, unannounced.

"Do you know who's manager now?" Donna Lee demanded.

He shoved the invoice, laden with the code for the homeland defense budget (well, yes, a burst sewer could be used to spread biohazards), behind his take-out sushi.

"Oh, Miss Keely," he muttered, halfway rising from his chair. "Do we have an appointment?"

Though she was no longer his boss, he still felt a little cowed by her. This was not right, he knew. After all, he was a full-fledged superintendent, someone way above her as far as the People page went in the Tula Springs *Herald*. But he never could forget the conversation he had overheard when he'd worked for her. She had been on the phone with a friend of hers, complaining about the men in Tula Springs, how homely they were. "My mother's always wondering why I never got married," Donna Lee had said, as he filed in the next room. "The real wonder, girl, is how any of the men in this town manage to find themselves a woman. You'd have to be on a three-day binge to marry a Pickens."

Yes, that was her phrase, "a Pickens." To this day, the wound still festered. Someday he'd like to tell this attorney a thing or two, namely that the woman he'd married hadn't been on a three-day binge. In fact, the woman didn't even allow beer in the house. Furthermore, it was Maigrite, not him, who had done the proposing. He would have been content carrying on that little affair they'd been having. But as Maigrite explained during her proposal, her husband was oiling up his shotgun, getting ready to come looking for Mr. Pickens if he, Mr. Pickens, didn't do the right thing by his wife. See, when Maigrite had told her husband she was pregnant and wanted a divorce, the husband said he could think of no better punishment for that shit-eating home wrecker—i.e., Mr. Pickens—than to have to marry the lying bitch he'd been fooling around with. So just a week after divorcing Emmet Orney, Maigrite married Mr. Pickens, who found out the following week that the gross of Pampers scented the staff at WaistWatch had gifted him with would have to find some other use around the house. False alarm.

"May I ask my assistant to fetch you some coffee, Miss Keely?"

"It's her landscaper, Burma's landscaper," she plowed ahead, not even acknowledging the offer. In her stone-washed jeans and peasant blouse, her fading blond hair frizzed by the humidity, she gave every appearance of being as tolerant as a folk singer's groupie. Good luck if you believed this, though.

"Listen, Pickens, do you realize that Schine is now the manager of Redds, Burma's boss?"

"Good lord. That's impossible. Why would he want to work there?"

"Travis told me that, I mean, Mr. Harper said, well, actually it was his wife, my *client* . . ."

Mr. Pickens studied her confusion a moment. "Yes, his wife, of course," he said, with a faint smile. Oh, how good this felt, to see Miss Keely tongue-tied, off balance, her eyes darting every which way for an escape. It confirmed something he had long suspected: This woman must be a lesbo. And as if this weren't bad enough, Miss Whole Earth was having an affair with one of her own clients: Mr. Harper's wife! Why else would Mrs. Harper leave a man as handsome and well proportioned as Mr. Harper—not that Mr. Pickens himself thought the accountant was well proportioned, of course. He had only heard that assessment from the mayor.

Yes, this explained everything. No wonder every man in Tula Springs looked homely to Miss Keely.

"As I was saying," Donna Lee resumed after plucking a strip of ginger off of Mr. Pickens's sushi platter, "Mr. Harper's wife, my client, was telling me that that foundation the landscaper works for—well, it's nothing but a T-shirt or two now. Just a scheme Dr. Schine's been cooking up, trying to raise money for."

Distracted by the limp ginger in her hand, *his* ginger, Mr. Pickens said, "Why does he want to turn everyone into dwarfs? Growth is where it's at."

She popped the ginger into her mouth. Only a lesbian would pop ginger like that, like some redneck trucker at a sushi bar.

"*Mrs.* Harper is sure the foundation doesn't really exist yet, aside from the T-shirts. She's worried to death that that landscaper is going to bilk Burma of every last cent she has."

Mr. Pickens held out the platter of yellowfin, California roll, and eel. Perched on the edge of his desk, she failed to catch the irony of the gesture. In fact, she actually stole his favorite piece, the Cajun eel.

"Curious, isn't it?" he said, shoving the platter as far from her as the desk allowed. "Why is *Mrs.* Harper so concerned about Burma's welfare? I never knew they were friends. Now, her husband, being Burma's accountant and all, him I could understand being upset."

Donna Lee's knuckles went white as she fondled his see-through pen. "Let's leave my client out of this, Pickens. If you knew anything about professional ethics, you'd know my relationship with clients, as well as with the people they're suing, is confidential."

With a shrug, the superintendent plucked the last yellowfin from the tray. *Very confidential, I'm sure,* he almost said.

"What's that?"

"Nothing."

"Anyway," she went on, "now that Schine has wormed his way into Redds, it's going to be that much easier for him to get at her dough. He'll have her financing that stupid foundation and diverting every last cent into his own pocket."

Mr. Pickens just sat there, staring off into space. These Zenlike moments usually occurred when he was confronted with urgent business. At such times Mr. Pickens had taught himself to escape into a mini-nirvana where nothing at all mattered.

"Well?" she prompted. "Say something."

The blank look on his face remained for a blessed moment or two. Then, refreshed, he dipped a roll into the wasabi's pert green.

"Speaking of campaigns, Miss Keely, I was wondering how your own is coming along."

"Who said anything about campaigns?" She yanked a leaf off his ficus—or at least, attempted to. It was plastic.

"Here you are trying to get me impeached—yes, I know all about it. Burma told me how you've been itching to get your hands on her money so you can run me out of Streets, Parks, and Garbage."

Donna Lee shrugged off her backpack and unzipped a compartment. "Must everything be about *you*, Pickens? Here I am pleading for my dear friend's very life, and all you can think about is your own stupid job. And by the way, it's Streets, Parks, and Sewers—not Garbage." She slapped a leaflet onto his desk. "Here. Take a look at this."

"CEGAR," Mr. Pickens read aloud. "And for your information, it's Garbage. They changed it to Garbage."

"Then why does it say 'Sewers' on the Web site?"

"Because our webmaster had herself a hissy fit and quit, that's why. Now just what am I supposed to do about this?" He tossed the leaflet across the desk. "Banning growth hormones isn't going to affect me any."

"No? Well, how would you like this foundation to be financed and run by Mrs. Schine?"

"He's married?"

Donna Lee left the backpack on his desk while she plopped into a canvas director's chair. "Not yet, Pickens. But any day now, I'm expecting Burma to come charging upstairs with the good news."

"You don't mean . . . It's impossible."

"Get your hand out of my backpack, please."

"He's much younger, and so handsome." He fingered the oatmeal canister crammed inside the netting. "At least, that's what some gals were saying the other day. No one that buff could be interested in Burma."

"Indeed? Well, on the happy day when the knot is tied, Pickens, you'll have only yourself to blame."

"Me?"

"Yes, Ma'am, you. Here you could have wound up with millions, living like a king, Pickens. There she was down on her knees begging you to marry her, and what do you do? You turn right around and marry a penniless prude who won't even let you have a sip of beer. I just hope you're satisfied."

Mr. Pickens pondered this a moment. Why *had* he turned a multimillionairess down? It didn't make sense. Was he really that idiotic, especially since he sort of liked her, too? Then he remembered.

"For your information, she didn't have a cent when she proposed to me, Burma didn't."

And she didn't have Maigrite's rear end either, he mused. Or, for that matter, a husband who was going to blast him straight to kingdom come if he didn't marry her.

"Ah, your family values, Pickens, they're truly an inspiration."

"I mean, I didn't love her."

"Nonsense."

"Well, I didn't."

"Who gives a shit? She loved you. That's the only thing that matters. And listen up, buster, if I were you, I'd get cracking before it's too late."

"What?"

"You heard me."

"Miss Keely, I'm sorry, but I happen to be a married man. And a Christian. I find it truly offensive that you'd think that I'd consider . . . What is it, Edsell?"

Mr. Pickens's assistant had poked his head in the doorway. Just out of college, Edsell was serving two years as an intern for Preach-Out America, which had paid his tuition at a branch of Liberty University in Las Vegas.

"I notice Miss Keely is here," the assistant said, giving her a little wave. "You want your floss now?"

In order to earn spending money, Edsell, who had majored in dental hygiene, hired himself out as a professional flosser. Mr. Pickens found this practice vaguely disgusting, but the mayor had forbidden him to make Edsell stop it this instant.

"Don't tell me you're a client, too," Mr. Pickens said, as Donna Lee heaved her backpack from the desk. *What a world we live in,* he mused, *when a graduate of Sophie Newcomb signs up for such a service.*

"It was a birthday present," Edsell said, as he snapped on a pair of rubber gloves. "Mr. Harper gave her a year's worth of flossing in her office."

Donna Lee got so red in the face that one of her oatmeal canisters popped out of the netting. As Edsell leaned over to retrieve it from the Astroturf, Donna Lee said, "I won't need any flossing today, Edsell. And it wasn't Mr. Harper. It was Mrs."

*Of course,* Mr. Pickens thought, with a smug smile as she trundled out the door. *Mrs.*

"You say something?" she demanded, turning suddenly on the superintendent, who just stood there, mute and innocent.

"By the way, Miss Keely," Edsell said, removing his gloves, "can I service you at ten tomorrow 'stead of noon? Mr. Fred needs a ride to the urologist."

"I'd rather not discuss that here, Edsell."

Mr. Pickens bowed graciously. "Good day, Miss Keely."

## Under New Management

hen Burma shoved open the door to Redds, three oatmeal canisters fell to the floor. "Good night!" she called out to the empty aisles. "Can't anyone give me a hand?"

Because the manager was on-site, Burma had felt free to make her rounds, collecting the IMPEACH PICKENS canisters Donna Lee had set out earlier in the day. The post office, McNair's Better Clothing, and the Jitney Jungle could be checked off. She would do WalMark, Southern Auto, and Isola Bella after work.

"Dr. Schine, will you please come help?"

"What's all the racket?" Mrs. LaSteele asked, swinging open the door of the manager's office.

"Mama, what are you doing here?"

"Covering for your boss. Another load of Zen gravel just come in for Graceland. He's got to supervise where they spread it. Now if you don't mind . . ."

But she did mind. Mrs. LaSteele not only had on a Redds uniform, but she had also appropriated the manager's official eyeshade. After collecting the oatmeal canisters that had fallen onto the sidewalk, Burma dumped them in an Irregular Panties bin for the time being and headed straight for Dr. Schine's office.

"Mama, you go on back home where you belong."

"Dr. Schine said—"

"I don't care what that man said. I'm the boss here, see. And I'm fixing to lay down the law once and for all. Just pack up and . . ."

A customer glided past the open door. Though she didn't use a walker, this customer was uncommonly massive. And yes, Ma'am, she was wearing a turban! Burma hurried out of the manager's office before the customer could get out the front door.

"Pardon me," Burma said, blocking the exit in what she hoped was a friendly way.

The woman's dusky face went hard as she clutched her handbag.

Burma smiled. "Did you come in here about a week ago and buy some clothespins?"

"Clothespins?"

"You have a daughter, don't you? I mean, granddaughter." Burma spoke slowly and distinctly, a little louder than normal, as if English were a second language for the customer.

"Wait here, Ma'am. Understand? Wait right here."

She patted the woman's plump beige hand before scurrying off to find her purse. She had set it down somewhere. Oh, but where?

"Mama, you seen my Fendi?"

Mrs. LaSteele looked up from the weekly inventory she was revising. "What? Quit messing up my papers. There's no Fendi here."

But there was a Celine Boogie Bag, her mother's.

"Daughter, you let loose of that."

"I just want to borrow a few dollars. I owe that customer out there . . . I mean Mr. Pickens owes her . . ."

"Pickens?"

"Her granddaughter is on the *Ronald Reagan,* and I don't know her name or anything so I just got to . . . Let go my hand, Mama!"

Burma wrenched free and hurried out of the store.

In her turban and billowing white smock, the customer was crossing the street majestically, not even deigning to look at the Eleuthra that had screeched to a halt, inches from hitting her. Burma thrust the cash into the woman's hand.

"Here, this is yours, dear. Take it. And don't show it to no one, not a soul—'specially Pickens. Just let this be our little secret, dear. Understand?"

Now that she was well-off Burma could eat anywhere she wanted. Or so you would think. The trouble was, Burma's mother was getting fussy. Mrs. LaSteele used to think it a treat to get the early bird at Dick's China Nights. But now she was even finding fault with Isola Bella, Tula Springs's fanciest restaurant.

"All right, Mama, so they put peanuts in the coleslaw. Just where do you want to go then?"

It was four-thirty, and Dr. Schine had still not returned to the manager's office. It was just the excuse her mother needed to stay put all day.

"Let's order in," Mrs. LaSteele said, picking up the phone. "I feel like chicken-liver croquettes."

"No one's going to deliver croquettes, Mama."

"Wanna bet?" Mrs. LaSteele's blue eyes twinkled as she tapped out a number.

Burma would have stopped her, but three customers were waiting at the cash register. She supposed she better see if they were trying to buy *Snow White*.

"Lord," she muttered, as she passed the Irregular Panties bin. Her Fendi was in plain view, right on top of a couple of oatmeal canisters. While the customers waited by the register, one muttering to herself about the help you get these days, Burma counted out the cash inside her purse. Yes, all there. $4,579 and change. And Mr. Pickens thought they needed a Code Orange system.

"Would you like a CEGAR T-shirt?" Burma asked after handing the third customer his change. He had bought an extension cord for $1.98 plus tax.

He just stood there, gazing blankly at her.

"It's free," she prompted.

" 'K."

He held out a meaty palm. Of course, there was a wedding ring. Seemed like every man she waited on had one of those things. And yet her mama still insisted this was the second-best way to meet men. It was the real reason Burma held onto her job at Redds, the hope of meeting an eligible customer. She hadn't had that much success with chat rooms, Lord knows. Despite the $36 million, the chat rooms were a big fat disappointment, romantically speaking.

If you overlooked the ring on his finger, you'd have to say that this customer did have a sexy little belly lapping over his belt, and he was about the same height as Mr. Pickens, too. But here he was, willing to accept a T-shirt without even knowing what it stood for.

"CEGAR?" he said when she confronted him on this score. "We got to keep that blame woman from taxing our smokes, right?"

"Actually, sir, I'm for the governor's tax. It'll give our teachers a raise."

He shrugged—or tried to shrug. The effort seemed to defeat him. Even Mr. Pickens at his dopiest could manage a shrug, Burma mused, somewhat mesmerized. This extension-cord consumer was so passive, such a round-shouldered, limp jellyfish, that he seemed to ooze a vague erotic charge.

"CEGAR stands for Center for the Elimination of Growth Hormone Research," she prompted after enduring yet another hot flash.

"Stem-cell shit, huh?"

"No, this is more like stopping people from getting too big. The earth has limited resources. Global warming is a fact, not a theory."

"Yeah? Well, here's a fact for you, lady: Suck it up and get with the program."

The wind chime over the door tingled as his cord trailed languidly behind him.

"Don't you know what yellow means?" her mother asked, tapping the flashing light beside the cash register.

It meant, of course, that all employees should report to the manager's office. Burma ignored it as she slammed the cash register drawer shut with the $1.98 plus tax. Triple tax, actually. And the dope didn't even notice.

"Look here, girl." Mrs. LaSteele plunked her bag down on the counter. "I'm missing almost a hundred dollars."

"Five hundred, Mama. That's what Mr. Pickens owes that woman in the turban. I'll pay you back, don't worry."

"Just why are you responsible for Pickens's debts? Tell me that."

Burma started to mention Ronald Reagan, but then ground to a halt. "I'm sixty-one years old, Mama. I don't have to explain myself to you."

Mrs. LaSteele's eyes blazed from the customer side of the counter. "I was hoping it wasn't true. I was hoping I had raised a child with values."

"I have values, Mama. I got so many values I'm about to dry up and blow away."

"What's that supposed to mean?"

Mrs. LaSteele had to crane her neck as if she were in New York, looking up at the Statue of Liberty. Whoever manned the cash register at Redds got a good foot or two added to her height because of the raised platform.

"Don't you know that Pickens is married? Doesn't marriage mean a thing to you, child?"

With the back of her hand Burma swiped at a tear coursing down her cheek. "Sure does, Mama. It means what everyone in this entire town's got but me."

"I want you to stop mooning over that man. Land's sakes, paying his debts, making him tea . . ." Mrs. LaSteele had rounded the counter and was leading her daughter away from the cash register.

"The whole town's talking about you and Pickens having tea."

"That was his idea, Mama. Not mine."

Mrs. LaSteele sat her daughter down on a floor model, a beanbag chair 30 percent off because it leaked garbanzos. "It's about time you came to your senses, girl. It's not going to be."

Burma took the lace handkerchief from her mother and blew.

"Even if he were available, Daughter, even if Pickens didn't have a good Christian wife to beat some sense into him, I still wouldn't let you near that man, not with a ten-foot pole."

Burma snapped the rubber band on her wrist. "Why not, Mama? He's a Republican, isn't he? You always wanted me to marry a Republican."

"Don't make me laugh. That man is about as Republican as Carter's Little Liver Pills." Mrs. LaSteele's fan alighted on her daughter's dimpled knee. "Now look here, Missy, I went to a lot of trouble to get your mind off that trash. You think it was easy convincing a Ph.D. to apply for this job?"

"Oh, brother, I should have known."

"Now there's a man for you." The fan, unfolded, covered the lower half of Mrs. LaSteele's wrinkle-free face with a panda. "You ever feel Dr. Schine's muscle, girl? A real man's man."

Burma sighed. For once her mother had got it right. Shortly after depositing his laptop in the manager's office, Dr. Schine had informed Burma that there would be no more mayonnaise coming between them. Though he had no ring, he was legally wed. His spouse, the football coach at John Alden College in New Hope,

Massachusetts, was a strict believer in monogamy and e-mailed Dr. Schine twice a day. Dr. Schine, you see, was researching red states, using Girardian triangulation to redefine the concept of legally blind—i.e., workers who guaranteed themselves a worse life by subsidizing incredible wealth. The data Dr. Schine had collected for his different fronts—CEGAR, among others—already confirmed one vector: Almost any campaign could be sold to SUV owners if a free T-shirt was involved.

"Mama, I wish you'd just give up," Burma said, her flush not cooled by the fan aimed at her now. "I'm never going to find myself a man, and that's that."

The fan went into high gear. "I ought to wash that mouth out with soap, young lady. Here the good Lord has served up a real hot-dog on a silver platter, and you sit there and whine."

Burma snapped the rubber band on her wrist. "Look, if this dog is so hot, why would he want someone like me? I'm old and fat and only got a B.A."

"Maybe so, but don't forget you also got yourself a hundred million. If that don't take off a few pounds, I don't know what will."

"Not a *hundred*! I wish everyone would quit saying that. I'm down to thirty-five, maybe not even that!"

The fan fluttered to a halt. "That all? Well, anyway, you don't have to blab that to Dr. Schine. Or let on you're sixty-one."

Burma held out her arms in a pose reminiscent of Jane Eaglen's Brunnhilde on the DVD overdue at the parish library, just before her horse collapsed into the funeral pyre. "Sixty-one! Hear that, everyone! Sixty-one! And I weigh exactly a hundred and fifty-two pounds, shoes off!"

"Hush that mouth!" Mrs. LaSteele yanked the rubber band off the arm extended in her direction. "Tacky as sin."

"Give that back."

"You think a Ph.D. is going to want to marry someone who snaps her wrist?"

"It doesn't have nothing to do with that rubber band, Mama!" she said, snatching it back. "It's the mayonnaise. I tried to get him to rub some off and he wouldn't. Ever since I hired him, he's stopped caring about my stain. I even ran out to the Jitney Jungle to get the Blue Plate he recommends, and when I come back with it, the kind with all the lipids in it, he tells me he's married and doesn't believe in nothing but monogamy. I hope you're good and satisfied, Mama, 'cause now I'm stuck here in this store all day long with a *monogamist!*"

Mrs. LaSteele's eyes hunkered down. More than once Mrs. La-Steele had consulted with her physician about the early warning signs of Alzheimer's. Ever since inheriting those millions, her daughter had exhibited disturbing symptoms of what had claimed Mr. La-Steele's reason long before she, Mrs. LaSteele, had divorced him. As a precaution, Mrs. LaSteele had already put down a deposit on a nursing home for her daughter.

"You're talking crazy, child. Get a grip."

Already smudged with mascara, the lace hankie couldn't soak up many more tears. "I'm going to die an old maid, Mama. You might as well get used to it."

"Easy, baby. No one can call you that even if you die right this very minute. Why, you already got one husband—remember Mr. Van Buren, all that free catfish you used to bring me?"

"Dead ones don't count, Mama. Let's face facts. You got yourself an old maid, a big fat old—"

"Hush!" Mrs. LaSteele cautioned as the wind chimes on the door tinkled. "Here's our croquettes."

The two women composed themselves so well that the delivery boy from Dick's China Nights noticed nothing but the lousy tip from the one with chopsticks in her hair.

# Put a Stop to It Once and for All

*M*r. Pickens had to see Burma. But it was harder than ever now, with the new manager installed over at Redds. Once, when he had seen Dr. Schine drive off in Mrs. LaSteele's new car, a MINI Cooper, Mr. Pickens had hightailed it across the railroad tracks and creaked open the delivery entrance in back. But instead of Burma, there was Mrs. LaSteele behind the cash register. While he pretended to be looking for some padded hangers for better trousers, Mrs. LaSteele dialed for help. Since he was the one delegated by AAA SecureAlert to respond to break-ins in the Third Ward, his own pager had gone off in the store.

In any case, the matter was now so urgent that he had no choice. He would have to meet Burma after dark, when there was less chance of being spotted.

"Isn't there a place we can sit?" Burma complained after five minutes of walking up and down the aisles. "My feet can't take it."

"Don't!"

But it was too late. She had appropriated one of the motorized carts WalMark had set aside for the disabled.

"Burma, get out of that thing."

"Why? I'm a taxpayer, aren't I?"

"One normal person," Mr. Pickens muttered to the lubricants he hurried past. "That's all I ask for, one normal person in my life."

"What is it you want to say to me, Bobby? I can't stay much

longer. Mama is bound to wake up and send a neighborhood watch out looking for me."

WalMark at 1:00 A.M. seemed like the safest bet to him. If they did happen to see someone they knew, they could easily drift apart. Besides, he was multitasking: He still had some Christmas shopping to do. It was already August, and usually he'd purchased most of his holiday gifts by March. But this year there were more folks on his list—i.e., all the staff at city hall who were mad at him for forgetting Secretary's Day. Never mind that not a single one of them was his secretary. They were all still prickly and sullen.

Mr. Pickens paused in front of an electric car-polish dispenser. This might work for his intern, who had reported him to the executive committee for not attending the daily staff prayer breakfasts at IHOP.

"Bobby!"

"What?"

"Answer me. Why the hell did you drag me out of bed at this hour?"

"Keep it down." He surveyed the next aisle, empty too. "I just want to warn you, Burma. Mrs. Pickens is on the warpath. You and I can't be seen together. Not for any reason whatsoever."

"Good! Suits me fine. Just give me back the five hundred bucks you owe me, and we'll call it quits."

He flapped his hand as if to dilute the sound waves. "Quiet, will you? Not so loud."

Her motorized cart hummed briskly past steering-wheel pads.

"Slow down. Now look. You made a really big mistake, Burma, trying to bribe Iman."

"What the hell you talking about?"

"Did you think she wouldn't talk? She went straight to Mrs. Pickens with the five hundred you gave her."

Burma's cart squeaked to a halt. "That nice clothespin woman works at WaistWatch?"

"No, the nice clothespin woman doesn't work at WaistWatch. You didn't give the money to her. You gave it to Iman, my wife's assistant. Mrs. Pickens had sent her into Redds to spy on you, and what do you do, Burma? You try to bribe her. Lord Almighty, how could you be so . . ."

"She had on a turban, Bobby, that's how."

"Just because someone's wearing a turban doesn't mean you have to give them five hundred dollars. Can't you tell one African American from another?"

Burma slammed a pint of STP into her cart's basket. She, too, was multitasking. "Look here, Carl Robert Pickens, I'm the least racist person you'll ever meet. Don't you dare tell me I can't tell any difference."

"Fine. In which case, you're now out a thousand bucks. Mrs. Pickens refuses to give back the five hundred she took from me. And her assistant is buying herself a trip to Sioux City with the five hundred you gave her."

"Sioux City?"

"Yes, she wants to see what Iowa looks like."

Burma, who was trying to remember if there was anything else she needed in Automotive, stared blankly at him for a moment.

"Well, that's Mama's money, anyway. I just won't repay her until you get the money back."

"Don't you understand, Burma? Iman isn't going to cough up a cent. Neither is my wife."

Perched in the cart, Burma couldn't help studying his crotch for a moment, a bulge to one side that could either be bunching undershorts or . . .

"Well, maybe the woman is poor. What does Mrs. Pickens pay her, Bobby?"

"There you go again, Burma, letting folks rob you blind. Don't you get it? Iman is a Republican."

Burma groaned.

"You've just handed over a thousand bucks to the Republicans, Burma. How do you like them apples?"

"Oh, Bobby . . ." Her face collapsed against the superintendent's lush seersucker folds and valleys.


On principle Donna Lee never set foot in WalMark. All her friends knew how much she loathed this cancer on the American landscape. Because of a contribution to the mayor's reelection campaign, the WalMark on Martin Luther King Jr. Extension had got its access road paved, courtesy of taxpayers' dollars. This was the crux of Donna Lee's campaign to impeach the superintendent of Streets, Parks, and Sewers. Martin Luther King, you see, wasn't even in the city limits. As if this weren't bad enough, the mayor had officially changed the name of the extension to Ronald Reagan Parkway.

So there could be no safer place for Donna Lee to meet Travis, Mr. Harper. She couldn't bear the thought that anyone she knew would see them together. Of course, Mr. Harper could have parked his car a block or two away from her apartment complex. But there was always the risk of someone's noticing him lope up the outside staircase. And the apartment itself, so cozy, the bed only a few yards from the living room sofa, well, she knew it would be impossible to end everything there. He was still too lovely to resist, especially after a glass of Oregon zinfandel.

No, in order to stop this thing once and for all, she needed to be in the most sexless place imaginable.

"Stop that," she said, snatching her hand away from his lips. "Don't you understand? We're history. Done."

His brown eyes magnified by tears, Mr. Harper gazed with bovine devotion across the table at her. They were the only customers at WalMark's EspressCafe. "Darling, I love you . . ."

"But give me Park Avenue."

"What?"

"Nothing." A little dopey at this hour, Donna Lee made a mental note to reduce her intake of *TVLand*.

"I've never met anyone like you, sweetness. You're so . . ."

"Stop. Just stop it," she said, not very convincingly. Yes, he did make her feel as fresh and green as a farm girl. Just being in his presence swept her back ten, twenty years. Oh, if only she weren't suing him at the moment, on behalf of her client, Mary Jo Harper.

Yet her concern wasn't about professional impropriety itself. Rather, about the *appearance* of impropriety. After all, because of their sporadic affair, Donna Lee had helped her client out enormously, getting Travis to agree to all sorts of conditions that his soon-to-be ex-wife would never have been ceded otherwise. Indeed, the Louisiana Bar Association should give her, Donna Lee, a citation for going the extra mile for her client.

Another aspect of the affair most people wouldn't understand was the environment. Thanks to Donna Lee, Travis was on the verge of believing in global warming. Once she got him to actually believe, Burma's checks to the Sierra Club would quit bouncing. Yes, he was always accidentally-on-purpose writing these checks using the old account number, the one Burma had when she was poor. Not only that, Mr. Harper agreed to feature a documentary on the destruction of the wetlands at the proposed IMAX. If Burma would only agree to donate Graceland to the AmStar Foundation, she could begin educating thousands of schoolchildren about conserving the wetlands.

"But why, Donna Lee? Why stop it? All I got to do is initial those clauses and I'll be totally legal for you."

"But you *haven't* initialed them yet."

It was his foot now, running up and down her calf. She twisted to the side in the booth.

"It's not fair, darling girl. Mary Jo has sucked every last cent out of me. And now she gets the children on Christmas day, too?"

"Your own fault, Travis. You had no business sneaking off to see that horrible woman last Christmas."

Mary Jo Harper was not the only one having a hard time forgiving Travis for that. At first, when Mary Jo had told her about this particular tryst, Donna Lee was sure the woman must have been mistaken. But then Mary Jo e-mailed digital photos taken at the benefit Travis had attended on December 26 in Alexandria, Louisiana. There he was with his arm around Maigrite Pickens at Clean Needles, a fundraiser for indigent executioners' funerals. And there he was with his hand on her tush as she opened the door to Room 103 of the Days Inn. Of course, he claimed he was just getting some voter preference forms for his First Baptist congregation.

The thought of this betrayal made it easier for Donna Lee to resist the man now. O.K., so she hadn't been dating Travis last Christmas. But the idea that he could find a woman like Mrs. Pickens attractive— a woman who glued reindeer onto her sweaters during Christmas— well, it was positively degrading. The very thought of Maigrite Pickens sitting so smugly in her office at that horrible Christian spa across the railroad tracks nearly sent Donna Lee over the edge.

"Oh, darling bug, it's not what you think," Mr. Harper said, as the waitperson topped off his coffee with a warm smile. "Mrs. Pickens was too drunk to do anything but talk."

"Sure, that's why she invited you to her room."

"I swear, she just wanted to complain, that's all. You know, Poop, life isn't easy for her. What if you had to be married to that husband of hers?"

As she reached into her backpack for an oatmeal canister, Donna Lee said, "No one made her marry Mr. Pickens."

"Actually, her husband at the time did. He said he was going to shoot Mr. Pickens if he didn't marry her. And furthermore, one of her legs is shorter than the other."

"You know something, I'm getting sick and tired of hearing that one of her legs is shorter than the other. Even that flosser you sent me, Edsell, won't shut up about that leg of hers. Don't you guys know that everybody has one leg shorter than the other?"

"Really?"

"No one has a perfectly matched set, Travis. So enough about that woman's leg."

"Well, at least you should feel a little compassion about the other thing, her husband."

"Why? Why should I feel one ounce of compassion for a woman who stole Pickens away from the one person on the entire planet who's chemically wired, Lord knows how, to find him lovable?"

"Who's that?"

"Burma Van Buren, that's who. Your dear client. As far as I'm concerned, Maigrite deserves all the misery that man can dish out."

Travis smiled up at the waitperson hovering beside the table, coffeepot in hand. "No more, thanks."

"I wish you wouldn't do that," Donna Lee said after the waitperson finally went back to the counter. He and Travis had exchanged small talk for almost five minutes, it seemed.

"Do what?"

"Flirt with everything on two legs."

Mr. Harper shook his head slowly. "The man's over sixty, Donna Lee. Maybe seventy."

"Did you see the way he was looking at you? He's in love with you, Travis. And you encourage him."

"You really are nuts, you know."

"He's gay, can't you tell?"

Mr. Harper shrugged. "How would you like to be stuck here serving folks all night long? You really are pretty hard-hearted, you know."

This stung. Here Travis Harper pals around with D.A.s and executioners, men who commit serial homicides, and he calls *her* hard-hearted. If she had any sense, she would get up right this moment and not even bother setting out any more canisters.

"Get that out of my basket!" Burma said as Mr. Pickens tossed another impeachment canister into the motorized cart's wire basket. "There's no room for my stuff now."

"So it's O.K. if that woman gets me thrown out of office?"

"I've been picking up Quaker Oats all over town, and you never once thanked me. Not once!"

"Keep it down, Burma."

They were both testy since the incident in Automotive. Burma had rubbed her cheek against something turgid in the seersucker and put her hand to his zipper. If it weren't for a sales associate who had rounded the corner with a pricing gun, who knows what might have happened.

"That must be it," he muttered, as he swerved past an aisle with a lone customer. "You want to ruin me."

Burma tossed the impeachment canister from her cart into the basket he was propelling.

"Did that woman put you up to it, Burma?" he said. "Is that why you tried to unzip me back there?"

"What the heck you talking about?"

"Miss Keely. She'll do anything. And if she can't do it legally, she gets her friends to . . ."

"To what?"

"Expose me in public, that's what."

For three aisles Burma was unable to speak. After all she had done for this man, defending him against Donna Lee's accusations (which were undoubtedly true), refusing to contribute a cent to the impeachment campaign, picking up canisters all over town—and now this, this was the thanks she got. Well, let him think what he liked. She was through with him. Finito, baby!

"How about a latte?" he said after several minutes of silent shopping. "Let me buy you a latte."

"Don't you dare try to be nice to me, Bobby Pickens." She was scanning her STP at a self-service counter. "Not after what you said."

From another self-service counter, where he was bar-coding a camel whose hump was guaranteed to sprout cumin, he muttered, "What? I didn't say anything."

"Your mind's in the gutter."

"*My* mind? Am I the one who hired a manager just because of his looks?"

"He's a Ph.D., Bobby." This comeback had to wait until the parking lot. Again, she had been too angry to speak at the time. "For your information, he's about twice as smart as you."

"How smart can he be to want to work in a two-bit bargain store?"

"You used to work there, Bobby."

"Yeah, but I didn't get a Ph.D. first." His shopping cart rattled over a speed bump. "O.K., fine, Burma, go right ahead. Let that dreamboat swindle you out of your last dime. See what I care."

She watched him unload the shopping bags into his Miata.

"I suppose it never occurred to you that Dr. Schine might be interested in me for any other reason, huh? Your mind just doesn't work that way, does it? You look at me and all you see is one great big dollar sign."

Mr. Pickens tried to hop into the Miata without opening the door, but a leg got stuck on the steering column. As Burma yanked him free, he said, "He's a good fifteen years younger than you, at least. Everyone's talking, Burma. Even Donna Lee. She thinks he's out to ruin you."

"She was talking to *you* about me?"

"As a matter of fact, yes. She came over to my office the other day to tell me how worried she is about your new boss."

Burma peered hard at the seersucker scrunched next to the gearshift. "Well, you just tell your dear friend she can stop worrying, since I haven't got a boss. No one bosses me around, Bobby Pickens. Including yours truly!"

"That man is going to take every cent you got."

"You're one to talk. When am I getting my thousand dollars back, Mister? I want my thousand dollars!"

With a misfire or two the Miata lurched onto the Ronald Reagan Parkway.

## Trouble in Paradise

*T*he Miata coasted to a halt. Mr. Pickens left his packages in the backseat and didn't even bother to lift the convertible top. Not the slightest sound could he afford to make.

He had worn his pajamas beneath his trousers and Perry Ellis sweater. After shedding the outer layer, he slipped into his twin bed. Safe and sound at last.

It would have been pleasant to lie there and savor having put one over on Mrs. Pickens. Except he wasn't sure what exactly he had put over. Clearly he hadn't had a good time that night. In fact, he was more vexed than ever. What could he possibly have meant by sneaking out of the house to try and reason with someone so mean and stingy? A thousand dollars? Yeah, right. Let her take him to small claims. We'll just see what Judge Vicki has to say about a woman who throws money at any turban that waltzes into Redds.

The smell of pork links woke him. Before he allowed himself to get too excited, though, he remembered that the WaistWatch brand was made from turkey wattles. Yet those were odorless.

In her frilliest apron, Mrs. Pickens greeted him with a curtsy as he paused in the kitchen door. "Grits or hash browns, Mr. P.?"

The hangover made it a minor chore to return her bright smile. His cottony tongue and throbbing head reminded him now why Wal-Mark had seemed such a reasonable idea last night. Yesterday, just before bedtime, when he couldn't find his Scope, he had gargled with her Listerine—or rather, as he discovered, Old Crow. The revelation that his wife was a secret drinker (along with a healthy dose of Chartreuse from his own secret stash in the Scope bottle he'd finally located) had given him the courage to sneak out. If she ever tried to accuse him of anything, he had his ace in the hole.

"You got any juice?" he asked.

"Fresh squeezed."

Like Julia Meade in the Kitchen of Tomorrow, she gestured toward the table. Fresh and elegant as a drop of dew, a single white rosebud peeked from a vase beside his coffee cup. But he didn't see any orange juice.

"Thanks," he muttered, a little perplexed.

"Drink up."

He picked up the empty juice glass and put it to his lips. This was all very nice. In fact, a little too nice. Usually on a weekday morning she only served a single cup of WaistWatch yogurt blend, which had to be supplemented at city hall by a few jelly doughnuts before the sushi she always ordered for his lunch was delivered.

"Silly," she said, pouring juice from a ceramic pitcher he hadn't noticed. It had been sitting behind a mound of pancakes oozing syrup. Not just syrup but his favorite kind of all—Mrs. Butterworth's!

"Dear, I really shouldn't be eating pancakes." With an unctuous smile, he patted the abs that WaistWatch's special-ed classes had failed to bust.

"You like pancakes, right? Then eat."

Was it his imagination, or did the pork links land on their best wedding china with a certain unnecessary vigor?

"Won't you join me?" he said, gesturing vaguely toward the other side of the table, which wasn't set.

She smiled brightly. "No, Iman and I have already had our yogurt this morning."

"Iman?"

"We've already walked five miles, Mr. P. She's showering now so we can head off to work, fresh as a daisy."

That was the rushing sound he had attributed to his hangover, a buzzing in his ears.

"Here? She's showering right here in this house?"

The smile was still like Julia Meade's, though maybe after twenty retakes on the set. "You got a problem with that?"

He swallowed. "No, I . . . Why is she here? Is something wrong at her house?"

"Stop squirming, Mr. Pickens. I just wanted company, that's all."

"Why now, this morning? I—listen, I really got to go. Do you think she'll be long in that shower?"

"Pardon me, sir,"—there was that curtsy again—"but someone has always been wondering why this house needs another bathroom. And I don't think that someone was me, dear."

"Yes, Maigrite, I agree. In an ideal world, two bathrooms would be very nice."

She was standing right over him with the sizzling cast-iron skillet. "More sausage?"

He held up a hand, meaning no.

"Oh, go ahead, Mr. Pickens."

She dumped the links on top of his pancakes, with only a few drops of grease splattering his boxer shorts. "You're getting everything else you could possibly want. A devoted maid at home and a little pork on the side, available any hour of the day or night. More coffee?"

Mr. Pickens put a tremulous hand over his cup. "I *really* got to go bad." The chair scraped across the linoleum as he got up. "So would you please ask your assistant to move it along?"

"Are you uncomfortable with an African American in your bathroom, is that your problem, Mr. Pickens?"

"My problem is I got to go. *Now*."

"You just can't stand having someone a little different around, can you?"

"Look, this has nothing to do with her. It's *me*! I'm about to burst!"

"I've always suspected you had a problem with coloreds."

"Yes, dear, I hate anything colored. Now that the truth is out, will you please get that woman to vacate the . . . ?"

But even if Mrs. Pickens had made an effort to free up the bathroom, it was too late. He bolted out the kitchen door.

In the backyard, where he was trying to find some relief behind the sweet olive, only a few drops would come out. Yes, he was aroused. He was feeling exactly what some pope had forbade, lusting after your own wife while trying to go number one. Well, at least he wasn't an RC. No sin was attached to this. Besides, was it his fault that all Mrs. Pickens had on besides that starched frilly apron was spike heels? Yes, nothing but those pointy heels! She must have been hitting the Listerine pretty early this morning.

"Mmmmmm Whffff!"

Startled, Mr. Pickens took a step or two away from the sweet olive. The neighbor's schnauzer had emerged from the undergrowth with a woof at the superintendent's turgid manhood.

"Get away, Edwin! Scat!"

Above him a full moon of a face had risen in the kitchen window, topped by one of his bleached towels. The whiteness of the temporary turban caught Mr. Pickens's eye as he hurried back inside.

## Confronting the Boss

*D*onna Lee's hybrid slowed as she neared Mrs. LaSteele's compact house. A pert MINI Cooper sat in the driveway, but there was plenty of room for her car, too.

In the noonday sun the lurid green of a sweet-potato vine almost blinded her. Dabbing at her eyes with a tissue, she rang the bell several times. No answer. She rapped on the door, then on the taut window off to one side. A glimpse of her reflection in a pane made her mutter something about her hair. As if to make up for the frizzing, she laid a breath strip on her tongue.

Something unreal about the green might have triggered it. Strange how artificial sweet-potato vines can seem. She had reached out to test a leaf and that was when it happened, the déjà vu. But it ended the moment he opened the door.

He looked thinner, almost reedy. Not quite as robust as that night she'd first seen him, after Bible study in her office.

"Excuse me, but I was wondering if I could sign up for a free T-shirt here."

Though the line was well rehearsed, Donna Lee faltered. A certain gesture of his had disarmed her. Was it the beautifully sculpted fingers combing through his jet-black hair? No man had ever displayed such grace, such a calm legato. In comparison, Travis—Mr. Harper—seemed such a clod. Yes, already she was being healed, finding some relief from that chronic ache.

"You know, the anti-tall thing," she prompted. "I've always thought everyone in Louisiana was too tall."

"Go to Redds. Ask for Mrs. LaSteele. She'll help you out."

"I was just there, but . . ." She smiled helplessly.

"I'm married, you know."

"Huh?"

"You're the lawyer upstairs from Redds, right? Burma said you'd probably be after me. So let me warn you, I'm not only married, I'm gay."

The truth, raw, unvarnished, landed like a sledgehammer on the brow of a pampered Kobe steer. Stunned, for a moment she couldn't even bleat out a protest.

"Are you insane?" she was saying a few minutes later, partially herself again. "Do you actually think a licensed attorney out to protect her client would be the least bit interested in a two-bit swindler?"

"Half and half?"

"Skim."

He rooted about in the refrigerator. Although every instinct had urged her to flee, she had stood her ground manfully. Indeed, how else could she prove her innocence to him, that she didn't give a hoot about his looks? That she was here on serious business?

"Mrs. LaSteele and her offspring don't seem to carry skim."

Donna Lee took a sip of the Lapsang souchong he had prepared. "They should, Dr. Schine. They really should. And by the way, I don't for one minute believe you're gay. Married, yes. But gay? A little too convenient."

"Nothing can be too convenient—honey?"

"It's Keely, Ms. Keely," she corrected before noticing the jar in his hand. "In any case, I just want you to know you're being watched, Dr. Schine."

He licked the excess from the jar, what had oozed out. "I've been stalked before. Usually by men, though."

"We are so vain, aren't we? I'm talking about a professional relationship here. I'm not going to let my client get bilked by you or any other con artist that comes down the pike. Burma told me you've already helped yourself to her mother's Escalade."

"Yes, I believe I've saved a few lives in this town. Do you have any idea how she drove that thing? She had to stand up to reach the brake."

"So where is it?"

He gestured toward the driveway. "Can't you see how much safer that little Coop is for her to drive? As a matter of fact, though, I try to drive her around as much as possible so she doesn't have to get behind the wheel."

"And who pocketed the difference, Dr. Schine?"

"The Food Pantry."

"What?"

"Mrs. LaSteele needed to give away that money or she'd be in another tax bracket this year."

"But that pantry is run by the Catholics. It's a crime to give those priests one red cent."

"Father Mike just volunteers there. They're actually funded by the Friends in Philadelphia. Honey?"

She guided the spoon away from her cup. "I said no, didn't you hear?"

"But you *do*, Blanche. You *do* take honey."

His smile, untroubled by any doubt, opened up a vast space in the cramped kitchen.

"At least, at WalMark you did."

"Huh?"

"Huh?" he mimicked, making her sound the perfect oaf. "What

indeed could the town's greenest citizen possibly mean by sipping tea at two A.M. with the Republican party chair? Who just happens to be Mrs. Van Buren's accountant, I might add."

"I never . . ." Somewhat dazed, she struggled to her feet. "You've got some nerve. I hate WalMark. Everyone knows that."

"My place?"

"What?"

"Dinner at my place tonight? Make it eight."

He handed her an oatmeal canister that had fallen out of her backpack as she tried to shrug it on.

"If you think for one minute that I'd ever set foot in your . . ."

"Ten thousand seven Cheryl Court. Now if you don't mind, I've got to get over to Graceland. Some yews have arrived."

As he breezed out the front door with a "Ciao," she felt for a moment as if this tiny house, crammed with the tackiest knickknacks, were hers. Yes, she had to suppress an urge to run after him, to explain that nothing here had anything to do with her—not the shepherdess simpering on the mantel, nor the matador swishing his neon cape on black velvet . . .

"Hold it right there, sister."

With a frown Donna Lee turned from the blinding light of the front door. In the hallway, murky as a cinema before your eyes adjust, a child advanced a menacing step or two, pointing something at her.

"Easy, sister, no false moves."

The voice was familiar. Of course, it was Mrs. LaSteele, who was no taller than a ten-year-old.

"Now, we're going to hand over that Vera Wang, aren't we, girl?"

"What? My blouse? It's Lands' End."

"The cup, sister, your teacup. Yes, that's right, set it right down. Now get those greedy little hands in the air while I dial for help."

Her eyes slowly adjusting, Donna Lee could now see the compact revolver. Or was it a cell phone the woman held to her ear, just below a chopstick?

"Mrs. LaSteele, there's no need to call anyone. I just dropped by to see if . . ."

"Hand me that phone," the woman said, as she took the snub-nosed revolver away from her own ear.

Donna Lee felt better once they had made the exchange, though she was still not happy about the call Mrs. LaSteele was making.

"Yes, she's holding a gun on me now," Burma's mother was saying into the cordless receiver. "The one I just bought at the Baptist auction to get us a new organ. The F-sharp was stuck."

"Mrs. LaSteele, please, it's just me, Donna Lee Keely."

"All my good china," the woman was saying at the same time, "and my Mini Cooper and . . ." Putting her hand over the mouth-piece, she said to Donna Lee, "Anything else? I'm calling my insurance man first, while it's still fresh on my mind."

Donna Lee pried the cordless away from her as politely as possible. "Look at me, dear. Can't you see who I am?"

"Darn tootin'. You're the shyster that's been preying on my daughter's poor weak mind. Shame, shame, Miss Keely. Here you con the poor child into writing checks to save some nasty old frogs when her mama's darling pooch is about to croak. Now you break into the mama's house to take the one nice thing she can call her own and—Oh, please, don't shoot."

Donna Lee was not aiming at her. She was just holding onto the revolver for safety's sake. Why, it was a crime for the Baptists to sell such a thing to an eighty-six-year-old woman.

"I can explain, Mrs. LaSteele."

"One more check goes out to those sick pinko frogs," the woman said, cinching her obi, "and they won't be the only thing endangered around here."

"All right, all right. Just calm down."

"Hands off my Burma's money, hear?"

"Relax, will you?" Donna Lee said, backing out the front door with the revolver.

Yes, she did hate people who laid rubber. But there were times when it couldn't be avoided, even in a hybrid. Donna Lee had to get over to the fund-raiser right this minute and give those Baptists a good piece of her mind.

## Who Prays for Sister Burma?

"*D*ID U XXX IN BUSH?" the text message read on his cell.

Mr. Pickens tapped out, "WHO IS THIS?"

It was Mr. Pickens's first prayer breakfast. Having a cell phone handy made his administrative assistant's intonements about God's guidance in city planning somewhat less numbing. Eight city hall staffers were crammed into a single curved booth. A receptionist's elbow jammed into Mr. Pickens's right side while his left cheek hung precariously over the edge of the vinyl ovoid. Mr. Pickens was the only superintendent saying amen this morning even though Edsell, his assistant, had assured him that the superintendent of Education always showed up.

"U PLEASURE USELF IN BUSH"

The screen on the cell phone blossomed with pixels of the sweet olive outside his kitchen window.

"Brother Bobby?"

He clicked his cell phone shut. "What?"

"Your offering," Edsell said with a pained smile.

Barely suppressing a groan, Mr. Pickens reached for his wallet. A nudge in the ribs corrected him. "Say something," the downstairs receptionist, a retired coroner who worked at city hall for nothing, hissed.

With the staff's assorted heads bowed a little closer to their Belgian waffles, Mr. Pickens murmured, "And when you pray, you shall not be as the hypocrites are, for they love to pray in houses of pancakes that they may be seen of men. But when you pray, enter into your own house and shut the damn door."

"Speak up," Edsell said from the head of the table, "we can't hear you down here. Tell us what you're offering up for Jesus today."

His mind in turmoil about the text message and photo—who could be sending him such trash?—Mr. Pickens resumed, "O.K., fine, I offer up my intelligence. I'm sick and tired of trying to make reasonable decisions based on facts, dear Lord. From now on, I'm going to rely solely on the mayor's direct pipeline to you. You told her the best way to raise revenue for the burst sewer main was to eliminate the free-breakfast program at elementary schools. Yes, Lord, as our mayor says, obese schoolchildren are also a health hazard. Two birds with one stone. Amen."

Three more offerings concluded the breakfast meeting, one from the receptionist, one from the new webmaster, and a heartfelt plea from the city attorney that every homosexual in Tula Springs get himself married. This last prayer caused a stir until the attorney, wiping powdered sugar off his nose, explained that he meant married to a female. "Find himself a good *female* wife, you dopes!"

His fleshy face beet red, the attorney threw down his napkin in the middle of Edsell's benediction and squeezed out of the booth with maximum commotion.

After everyone settled down, Edsell resumed his prayer. "As I was saying, Jesus, we most earnestly pray that Sister Burma escape the clutches of the evildoers that do plot to raise our taxes. Let Sister Burma join the ranks of the godly by offering up Graceland to the IMAX that will reveal, once and for all, whose side you're really on. Amen."

On his way out of the IHOP Mr. Pickens tried to veer away from his administrative assistant. But the intern was too quick for him. Though he was barely twenty-three, Edsell's lantern jaw and narrow-set eyes gave him the spry, wizened look of an octogenarian. Mr. Pickens felt an almost physical repulsion for this skin-and-bones hygienist who pried into oral cavities up and down Flat Avenue.

"The best, Brother Bobby. Yours was the best prayer of all."

Long ago Mr. Pickens had given up trying to get Edsell to call him "Superintendent."

"Beg your pardon?"

"Offering up your intelligence. It was a wise decision. By the way, did you hear what happened yesterday at the First Baptist gun auction?"

Mr. Pickens squeezed into his Miata with a wince. The steering wheel he had grabbed for leverage was broiling hot.

"I'm in a hurry, Edsell."

"My client tried to sell them a stolen gun."

"What client?" Mr. Pickens switched on the ignition.

"My four o'clock floss, Miss Keely. She broke into Mrs. La-Steele's house, stole the gun the old lady had bid on, then tried to sell it back to the First Baptists."

Mr. Pickens revved the engine while waiting for the steering wheel to cool. "Why are you telling me this nonsense? Don't you know Miss Keely doesn't believe in the Second Amendment?"

The administrative assistant shrugged. "Just trying to help, Brother Bobby. I mean, she is trying to get you impeached, you know."

Mr. Pickens slammed the gearshift into reverse. "Yes, I do know. And I'd appreciate it, Edsell, if you would refrain from eating oatmeal at your desk."

"Oh, don't worry, Brother Bobby. It's not Quaker Oats. It's state oatmeal from the school breakfast program. I'm entitled to eat as much as I want. You are too, by the way. It'd be much better for you than those jelly doughnuts I haven't mentioned to Mrs. Pickens when I do her ten-fifteen."

"What? You're flossing my wife?"

Edsell gazed benignly over the superintendent's head at the bigger picture. "I do everyone at WaistWatch, the entire staff."

"I'm telling, Edsell. I'm telling the mayor what you're doing on government time."

"Save your breath, Brother Bobby. She knows. I do her first thing in the morning, every day. That's when she hears what the good Lord has to say about city hall."

The steering wheel was still hot, but Mr. Pickens was even hotter as he backed the car as far away from that intern as possible. Some day, if it was the last thing he did, he would get that boy fired.

## The Eye of the Needle

*T*he gate would not budge for her. Furious at such nonsense, Donna Lee strode back to her hybrid. But before she opened the door, a voice crackled, "Turn around, Ma'am."

She looked at the bricks that flanked either side of the gate.

"Turn and identify yourself, Ma'am."

"Who is this, anyway?" Donna Lee demanded into the intercom, which she'd finally spotted amid the pansies that softened the un-tempered red of the brick wall.

"Do you have a password, Ma'am?"

"I'm here to see Dr. Schine. He lives on Cheryl Court."

"You'll have to get a password from your party, Ma'am."

"What?"

"Please enter your password, Ma'am."

Donna Lee assumed the pose she'd learned courtesy of Waist-Watch's 7:05 A.M. kickboxing class. Yes, she was enrolled at the hated spa, mainly because it was so convenient, right across the railroad tracks from her office. The only secular gym in town was way out by WalMark.

"Better buzz me in this instant, *Ma'am*," Donna Lee said, with a reverse flying crane, "or I'll . . ."

A hiss on the dented intercom gave way to a perky ". . . and two Whoppers with a Snickers Frosty. Would you like that super-sized?"

"Huh?"

"Please drive up."


10007 Cheryl Court greeted her with a monstrous garage. Indeed the living quarters seemed a mere cyst on an enormous body. Given months of study, no architect could possibly come up with a more un-sightly design. It was the norm for almost every house in Cherylview Estates, which Donna Lee had finally managed to gain entry to. As Dr. Schine explained a few moments later, the security gate was elec-tronically monitored from Colorado Springs by Halliburton, which also had a contract for take-out orders at ninety flood-prone Burger-Mats. Donna Lee's flying crane had apparently jarred the system into the take-out mode, which automatically opened the gate.

"Why anyone would choose to live here is beyond me," Donna Lee said, refusing the Cosmopolitan he held out to her.

"An excellent opportunity for me."

He was stretched out on a quilted sofa that curved into the middle of the living area. The florid ottoman where Donna Lee perched supplied the dot to the sofa's question mark.

"I'm surrounded on all sides by nouveaux riches," he went on with a barely suppressed yawn. He had greeted her at the door clad only in khaki shorts and a T-shirt. "They're far more primitive than the Ngobs I once lived among."

"Ngobs?"

"A riparian tribe with twenty-seven different words for a honey-comb. The headhunter who lives next door to me here . . ." He gestured toward the festooned drapes lavishly blocking out a security light that had nearly blinded Donna Lee as she waited for him to answer the chimes. "He's fond of repeating a single word with no meaning whatsoever. Hopefully, he says, the petrochemical firms will hire the CEOS he drums up for them."

Donna Lee's smile was uneasy. Though the room was huge, twice the area of her entire apartment, it seemed so confining. A massive entertainment unit built around a giant TV screen blocked any sense of flow.

"How can you bear living here, Dr. Schine? I'd go nuts."

"No worse than the mud wahli the Ngob elders housed me in."

"Really?"

He put a finger to his lips. "Well, actually, it *is* worse." His foot nudged a rack of DVDs. "Not a single book in the entire house."

"You're renting?"

"Not exactly, just a guest for a few weeks, until my research is done."

"But surely you must have brought some books of your own."

"Against the rules, Keely. I always go native, give myself no re-sources beyond what your neighbors' natural habitat offers.

"*My* neighbors? I've never even been in this part of town before."

Manicured lawns, one swollen garage house after another, and not a single mature tree. It was truly appalling.

"I meant Tula Springs, Keely. Burma told me you've lived and worked here your entire life."

"I didn't go to school here, and besides, Burma has no business discussing me anyway—not with the likes of you."

With a languid hand dangling over the edge of the sofa, he tapped the keyboard on the floor.

"What was that?" she demanded.

" 'The likes of.' Just entering it into the lexicon."

Donna Lee had never used that phrase before. It was something her mother would say. But when she tried to explain this to him, it came out garbled by rage.

"Sorry, man." He held up his hands. "Didn't mean to diss you or anything. But you *are* a native."

"You don't happen to have a bone lying around, something I could screw through my nose?"

"You were born here, right? At least, that's what Burma told me."

Donna Lee took a deep breath. "For your information, I spend most of my time doing pro bono work for the indigent. And I'm do-ing everything I can to get those crooks out of city hall before they turn Tula Springs into one big chemical dump." Her voice was mea-sured, affectless, even if her hands trembled so badly they had to be clasped together in her lap, as primly as a maiden aunt's. "So I would appreciate it if you would stop lumping me together with . . . And who told you I was at WalMark anyway?"

"Does it matter?"

"Yes, lies matter. They matter a lot."

She was still uncertain whether to admit the truth or not. That was the point of this visit. To find out how much he knew about her and Travis, Mr. Harper. And who could have told him.

He lolled back full-length on the quilted peonies of the sofa. "Well, if you must know, it was the woman you robbed."

"Yes, go ahead, smile." Unable to resist any longer, Donna Lee reached for the Cosmopolitan on the coffee table. A sip or two might help keep her eyes from straying to those bare legs of his, slick and cool as an early Rodin. "You leave me in a house with a loony eighty-six-year-old and a revolver. Thanks a lot, Dr. Schine. She nearly shot herself trying to call her insurance agent."

"I didn't know she had a gun."

"And the First Baptists wouldn't refund the money. They told me I had to give it back to her. She had a constitutional right to it, and they need a new organ."

"Didn't give it back to her, did you?"

"Of course not."

"Where is it, then?"

"None of your business. And neither is Burma Van Buren. She is my client, Dr. Schine, and I have a professional duty to protect her assets from people who get suspiciously cozy with her mother."

"Who told me you were at WalMark with her daughter's accountant."

Donna Lee took another sip. "Since when does an eighty-six-year-old make it a habit to shop at two in the morning?"

"So you admit you were there, Keely."

"I'm admitting nothing to you, Schine. Other than that I've been trying to work out some strategy with Mr. Harper to get Pickens removed from office."

"I see. By the way, I like your thing."

"What thing?"

Having just come from the courthouse, where she'd been suing the city for allowing raw sewage to leak into the courtyard of a low-income housing project, she was dressed in her most conservative outfit. Black pumps and a charcoal linen suit with her hair pulled into a severe chignon.

He tapped his throat.

Her mother's brooch, that was what he meant, a cameo that Judge Brown, who was trying her case, had given to her mother when they had gone steady in high school.

"Here in the jungle, Schine, we call this 'thing' a brooch."

"Why would Harper want Pickens impeached?" he went on, as if he hadn't heard. "I don't follow."

"Because he's giving Republicans a bad name."

"I see. So you're helping the Republicans clean up their act."

Glowering, she hoped her countenance was dark with menace. But apparently not. For he continued to loll on the overstuffed sofa, scratching his belly, which was smooth as an ice sculpture on a Carnival cruise.

"Are you as dumb as you pretend to be?" she said, setting down the empty glass. "Do you really think I'd want to help those people?"

This was where she should get up and exit, trailing her offended dignity. And she would have, too, if only he were slightly less gorgeous. Yes, one little flaw and she'd be out of there.

"Hm, let's see. I have a copy of the official log right here."

"Log of what?"

Still reclining, he fished through some papers on the hunt table behind the sofa. "Here we go. 'Neighborhood watch two-three-fifteen. Missing daughter reported by Mrs. G. LaSteele. Patrol car dispatched to Pickens's house for suspect husband. Mrs. Pickens answers door. Checks every room in house. No sign of husband. Mrs. P. distraught. Refreshes mouth with Listerine.'"

"I don't see what this has to do with me, Schine."

" 'After reconnaissance trip to WalMark, Minuteman Jane returns with Mrs. LaSteele to aforementioned's domicile. Daughter, Mrs. Burma, in bed asleep. When wakened, Mrs. Burma reports that mother's mind wanders. Daughter not missing. Case closed.' "

"No," Donna Lee said, as he held out the pink sheet toward the ottoman. "I don't need to see that. I already told you I was at Wal-Mark. What's the big deal?"

He folded the sheet a few times. "The big deal is thirty-six million dollars, Keely. Mrs. LaSteele is convinced that you and Mr. Harper are out to bilk her daughter of every cent she has."

A pink paper airplane sailed across the room. They both watched it take a nosedive after hitting a signed limited print of a camel smoking.

"Mrs. LaSteele has retained me to make sure this doesn't happen. Harper is not getting his hands on a cent."

"Mr. Harper is just trying to help with her IRS problem, Dr. Schine. If Burma donates Graceland, that would be settled once and for all. Besides, he's thinking about an IMAX that would educate children about global warming."

"Indeed? And what about the prisoners?"

"What prisoners?"

"Harper's planning to lock up antiwar protesters in the theme-park prison. They'd be dressed up to look like they won't fight the Spanish. Furthermore, AmStar is just a money-laundering operation. That's what Mrs. LaSteele herself told me. The money will actually be funneled to a PAC that—"

Donna Lee was on her feet. "How can you believe a word that woman says? Mrs. LaSteele herself is a known Republican."

"Yes, she is, but she's the rock-solid kind. Won't give a cent to anyone, not even the party, unless it lowers her tax base. I trust her.

But you, you're something else, Keely. Harper's wife is a client of yours, I believe. Is that why you were seeing him at WalMark? To work on an out of court settlement?"

"How dare you impugn my professional—"

"I'm surprised you didn't use that angle, Keely. It's a much better cover story."

A buzzer sounded. She gave a start, looking over her shoulder at the front door.

"Just my timer. The duck is done. You do eat duck, I hope? Terrific orange sauce I made. And you can pick out a good bone afterward."

*Part Two*

## A White Elephant

*N*o light is as tender as winter light. And no winter light could compare to that slanting on Tula Springs at 3:05 P.M. on January 18.

Greened by the Austrian pines, the rays transfigured their weary bodies. To her it was like being caught up in a nocturne made trite by countless amateurs. Yet now a master played in the waning afternoon, the inner voices singing under his pliant hand.

In the distance the columns loomed serene. Finally in place, the landscaping now modulated the brash Elvis theme into a bitter memory, not without its sweeter pangs.

The Zen stones they had crunched over were silent as they paused for a view of the house, the white elephant that still wasn't sold. Or donated.

Toward an artful arrangement of junipers they strolled. Each step offered a slightly different view of the columns. Her grounds could not be numbered or contained, she discovered. They held infinite promise.

While he gazed at the ivory glow on the faint rise of the horizon, she studied him. This silence, this light, was enough.

"Are you cold?"

"No, don't." She wouldn't take his jacket. "Keep it on yourself, Bobby."

Oh, how lovely he was like this. Impeached. All the starch knocked out of him. The man she remembered so dearly from the old days—lost, baffled—had returned.

"I still don't understand," he muttered, as they rested on a granite bench installed by Dr. Schine. "They told me there was no way the vote would go against me. The mayor herself told me."

"Stop obsessing, man. Let it go."

"Those new machines the mayor put in, I know they must be defective. There's no paper record, Burma. Mrs. Pickens herself, she told me when she went to vote, she pressed 'yes' in favor of impeachment and it came out 'no' on the screen."

Burma chafed his mittened hand. "O.K., listen to me. If the machines cheated in that direction—as I'm sure the mayor intended—it still doesn't help your case. Think, Bobby, you probably got more support than you deserve."

"Why must you be against me all the time? Just for once I'd like to hear a yes from you: Yes, Bobby, you got a point."

Hunched in misery, he had wrenched his hand free, leaving the mitten behind.

"You're taking this too hard. It's not like you're the first person to ever get impeached."

He stuffed his hand deeper into the pocket of his beige parka. "Yeah, but *he* was a Democrat. This is supposed to be a red town, Burma. How could folks turn against one of their own?"

"Well, those books Maigrite turned over to city hall didn't help."

"What books?"

Burma blinked innocently. "Your dear Christian helpmeet rounded up all the books you'd hid around the house, Molly Ivins, Al Franken."

"Those were *your* books, not mine."

"That was the other problem, Bobby. Me. All the exit polls said this impeachment was about values."

"Goddamnit, I have more values in my little finger than any of those morons."

"Of course you do. But there was always the appearance of moral laxitive. Everyone in town believes you and me were having a thing."

His eyes bulged with thyroidal passion. "But we weren't! We never did a thing!"

Burma sighed. Yes, he was right. They never had done a goddamn thing.

"Your mama has the biggest blabbermouth."

"Mama didn't have nothing to do with this." She slapped his mitten on the Vermont granite. "It was your wife. *She*'s the one."

"Yeah, but it was your mama woke up Mrs. Pickens that night and made her suspect something was going on."

"Look, Bobby, it wasn't my idea to meet you at WalMark at one in the morning. And Mama never did catch me. I got home to bed before she came back with the neighborhood watch. If you were dumb enough to confess to Maigrite that you'd run out Christmas shopping in August . . ."

"I never told her I was gone. Your mama had already woken Mrs. Pickens up before I got home. See, it *was* your mama. She's always had it in for me, from day one."

"Well, it wasn't Mama who sent that video of you in the sweet olive all over town." This she said as they tested the ice on the edge of the catfish pond. Burma had been too angry to go on talking on the bench. It wasn't until they had stood up to continue their inspection of the grounds that she got her voice under control. She just couldn't stand anybody criticizing her mother, especially when that anybody was right.

"Isn't that against the law, Bobby?"

"What? Going to the bathroom outside your own private domicile?"

"No, I mean filming someone pleasuring himself with a Palm Pilot. Couldn't you sue Iman for phoning that clip of you to Edsell?"

"There was no pleasuring going on, Burma! How many times I got to tell you? It was number one, plain and simple."

"Get back, Bobby. You're too far out."

"Anyway, if I took Iman to court"—his arms were outspread like a tightrope artist's as he crunched over the pond's ice—"she would get Mrs. Pickens to play that tape for the judge."

"What tape? Oh, where you say you hate coloreds?"

"I was dying to go to the bathroom. It was a joke. How did I know there was a microphone in that rose?"

"Well, I for one never joke when I got to pee. What was she taping you for anyway?"

"What in the hell do you think, Burma? A settlement. Mrs. Pickens wants to make sure I don't have a cent left after the divorce."

From a thicket of Chinese tallow came the angry chirp of a titmouse. Burma gazed vaguely in its direction while saying, "So that's where Edsell got the sound bite for his Web site. Sure didn't do you much good."

"Actually, it won over the city attorney. He voted against my impeachment."

"I always suspected that man must be prejudiced."

"No way, Burma. He goes duck hunting with a Yankee Italian—Justice Scalia. No, the city attorney told me he just couldn't help admiring anyone as politically incorrect as me."

"But you're not, Bobby. If you were that incorrect, you'd never have gotten impeached. I think—Oh, watch out!"

As his foot crunched through the ice, she gave him a yank that landed him in a clump of stubbly cattails.

"You O.K.?"

"Let go."

He wrenched his arm free. But he wasn't able to get up—mud gooed the reeds—until he finally took hold of her hand again.

Inside Graceland she urged him to get out of his wet trousers pronto. But he didn't feel like going all the way upstairs to his bedroom. Yes, ever since Mrs. Pickens had thrown him out of his own house, Mr. Pickens had been living in Graceland as caretaker—rent free with a small stipend in cash every week from the proprietor's accountant. Deducted from the stipend was the five hundred dollars Mr. Pickens hadn't stolen from the woman in the turban. So despite having been impeached, he still managed to scrape together a living.

"Just use the elevator, Bobby."

"It's broke. Only goes down."

"Well, whatever you do, don't get it fixed."

"I already called Otis."

"Bobby, I'm not going to pay a fortune to have that thing fixed. You can darn well use the stairs. Might do you some good."

But it was she who trudged upstairs clutching the curved banister. In the master bedroom she unhooked one of Mr. Van Buren's smoking jackets from the motorized clothes hanger. Silk pajamas were unearthed from an astragal-glazed secretary crammed with magazines she'd asked Mr. Pickens to recycle.

"Put these on, Carl Robert, before you catch your death!" she shouted from upstairs.

"What?" he said as the silk parachuted down toward him.

"Are you going to recycle Mr. Van Buren's muscle-car magazines or not?"

"I can't hear. There's water in my ear."

"Don't make me ask you again, Bobby Pickens," she grumbled as she headed for the sauna. She really needed to get the chill out of her bones.


## Shades of Delight


*A*ll Donna Lee wanted was a shade for the brass pole lamp in her office. Not a single place in town had the right size, not even WalMark, which she refused to set foot in usually. This explained why, busy as she was these days, Donna Lee had driven nineteen miles into the middle of nowhere to an outlet that claimed to be the largest bathroom-fixture store in the world. Though she had no literal belief in this billboard, Donna Lee went the extra miles because Burma had told her they had an annex that sold lampshades, every variety you could possibly imagine.

The clerk inside Slocum's Tub-A-Rama squinted up at Donna Lee a moment before saying, "No, lady, we don't sell lampshades. This here's for stuff you put in your bathroom."

A slight pulse in her belly worried her. She knew she shouldn't have drunk that Morning Thunder on an empty stomach.

"What about a restroom?" Donna Lee demanded as a cramp twisted her innards.

He led her to Section 12, where he snapped his sandals together and saluted. Scores of toilets of every shape, size, and hue were lined up for inspection.

"The friendly environment ones are in back. The super capacity are—"

Trying not to gnash her teeth, she managed to explain.

"Oh, you're talking about a ladies' room, one of them."

"You got it, Einstein."

"No ladies' on-site, Ma'am. They's a Conoco the other side of Liberty, only you got to fill up first, a full tank."

Cramping, Donna Lee emerged with a slight spurt out of the freezing outlet. For a moment she thought about using her hybrid as a shield, going behind the opened door. But a motorized cart marked SECURITY was heading right for her car.

A clump of willows not far from the edge of the asphalt beckoned with a few lone silvery leaves.

No one could see her from here, she reassured herself as a skink plopped off a decaying limb. She had unbuttoned her jeans and was about to scoot them down when she heard, "Listen, I need to make an appointment. Will you be in at four-thirty this afternoon?"

Maybe it was just someone talking on a cell in the nearby parking lot. Silent, wary, Donna Lee made no move.

But then the underbrush parted with a brittle crackle, and there she was, the brazen voice embodied.

"Well? You free at four-thirty or not?"

Just the other day Donna Lee had come across a photo in the manager's office at Redds. It featured a coarse-looking older woman with a toothy smile, blotchy complexion, and dark roots in her bleached hair. She had asked Dr. Schine if this was his mother. He had laughed, a laugh so delightful that she couldn't help joining in—until she recognized the cable-knit sweater. Her own. Yes, that was her, a Polaroid snapped by Burma at Redds's Christmas party.

"Cat got your tongue?" the woman demanded.

It was the photo all over again. Or rather, a negative. This woman was dark, a deep olive complexion, blotch-free. The pinched nose, the sharp chin and deep-set eyes, all so utterly alien. Yet at the same time, in an uncanny way, so familiar.

"You talking to me?" Donna Lee said.

The woman's mittened hands burst from the pockets of her red coat with an alarming jangle. Silver bells were knit into the even redder mittens that sawed the air for emphasis. "What are you doing out here anyway? Trying to find some three-legged frog, I suppose. Well, never mind that. Just tell me if four-thirty is O.K."

A sonorous cramp deep in her bowels launched Donna Lee into a panicked flight through a veil of dried-up trumpet vine.

"Hey, wait up!"

It sounded like an entire posse behind her, crashing through the underbrush on delicate hooves. Stumbling over a root, Donna Lee would have twisted her ankle if she weren't laced into her hiking boots. This was the limit. She whipped around with all the fury of a bayed vixen.

"Who are you? What do you want?" was all she could manage to say, though.

It took a moment for her pursuer to catch her breath. Thin, almost anorexic legs jutted from beneath the red cloth coat. Miraculously, the woman's spike heels didn't sink in the wintry muck polished by a brief bout of sleet.

"An appointment, Miss Keely. I want to divorce that no-good two-timing bum."

Of course. It was Maigrite Pickens, the woman who had seduced Travis, Mr. Harper, last Christmas at the Clean Needles fund-raiser in Alexandria. The woman who worked in that horrible Christian spa that was dunning her for two bonus kickboxing lessons. Didn't those morons know "bonus" meant "free"?

"Please go away. Leave me alone."

"Listen, Miss Keely, I'm sick and tired of getting the short end of the stick." Bells tinkled as a mitten thumped a reindeer appliquéd to the red coat. "I deserve the very best, and you're it, girl. You kick ass, the divorce lawyer that takes no prisoners."

"Please, I'm not really that good. Go away."

"You got that sucker impeached, Miss Keely, and now you're going to sue that boy for every cent his girlfriend has. For starters, he's going to buy me a second bathroom with the spare change that pork barrel's slipping him. I'm getting me a spa tub, top of the line."

"I'm sorry, Mrs. Pickens. But I can't."

"Sure you can. Let's get out of this cold, girl, and I'll show you the one I have in mind. It's got a sound system and different-color lights that change your mood automatically."

Donna Lee plucked a burr off her parka. "I've got far too many clients as it is. I don't have time for—"

"Watch out!"

Donna Lee staggered as Mrs. Pickens gave her an unnecessary shove. The security cart that had bumped into the woods stopped in plenty of time.

"Maigrite Pickens," a voice intoned from beneath the cart's green awning, "leave that woman alone. Young lady, hop in."

A plump hand, mellow as bladdernut, patted the molded plastic seat.

"Where you taking her?" Mrs. Pickens demanded as the cart drove off with Donna Lee, so desperate for escape that she had hopped aboard, no questions asked.

·   ·   ·

After escorting her through the security check at the Employees Only entrance, the guard ushered her to a restroom.

When Donna Lee emerged, she could barely resist an urge to throw her arms around this woman, the relief was so great.

"By the way," Donna Lee said, as the cart hummed toward the main parking lot, "you really ought to let customers use that restroom."

"They do, Mum."

"But that clerk told me I had to go all the way to Liberty, to a filling station."

The security guard grinned so wide it was almost audible. "That be Gary, I figure."

"Short, sort of chubby."

A smooth powerful hand slapped the steering wheel. "That boy, he is the hoot."

"What?"

"Poor thing get him so bored, he fool with the customer mind—especially ones do treat him bad."

Donna Lee's face darkened. "I was perfectly nice to him."

"Did he have this accent, real country?"

"Well, it wasn't exactly the BBC."

"So you know, Mum, that boy be a postdoc from Wisconsin."

Donna Lee glanced sharply at the guard, who was looking straight ahead without a glimmer of irony.

"What the hell is he doing down here selling tubs?"

"The dean at St. Jude, she just shut Philosophy down for the attempt to unionize. He write on Étienne Gilson while he wait to see if the unfair-labor-practice suit go through."

The cart halted abruptly as a Tundra pulled in from the highway.

"Well, I'm delighted he's so smart, but he still had no right to torture me like that, showing me toilets when he knew damn well I was dying."

"You must rub him the wrong way."

"Look, I happen to represent the Kant specialist in that suit. He didn't have to pick on me. All I wanted was a simple lampshade, and now it's nearly three-thirty, and I haven't accomplished a damn thing all day."

"See any you liked?"

Donna Lee smiled wanly. "You kidding?"

"It is not a bad collection, Mum."

"What? You mean there actually is an annex? But that clerk said . . ."

The cart swerved so sharply that Donna Lee felt herself impressed on the guard's powerful shoulder.


Just a few moments later the cart pulled up in front of an ancient Illinois Central railroad car nestled behind the outlet. The orange-and-brown passenger car, complete with bamboo shades, evoked a sudden pang of nostalgia. Years ago this very car had stopped at the railroad station in Tula Springs. How wild with excitement the Panama Limited used to make Donna Lee, barely a teenager then. Headed south, it would end up in New Orleans. But even more thrilling was the other direction, when it might carry you into a Chicago blizzard. Now there was no train at all, no station. Just the WaistWatch spa.

Donna Lee shoved open the weighty door.

So Burma wasn't crazy after all. The car was filled with lampshades, nothing but lampshades. But who in her right mind would travel all the way out here for lampshades? How in heaven's name did they stay in business?

"Yes, this is it," Donna Lee said, as she spotted the shade. "This is exactly it."

The security guard, who had followed her inside, peered at the price tag.

"Listen, how did you know I was dying out there?" Donna Lee asked the guard.

"One look at you running like a jackarabbit into those woods, Mum, I know it must be Gary again. Couple time a week the rich head for the woods. Gary has a problem with the rich."

Donna Lee tapped the shade she'd been admiring against her jeans and hiking boots.

"Do I look rich?"

"You sound it, Mum. And you got the look in your eye, real scrunchy tight."

Donna Lee sighed as she clomped over the plank flooring toward the cashier.

"Well, for your information, I'm not rich. As a matter of fact, you've hurt my feelings."

"No offense, Mum."

With some effort, Donna Lee took that as an apology. "Can you believe that woman followed me right into the woods? She must be nuts."

The guard made a thoughtful sound. Massive, squat, this guard nonetheless seemed a picture of health. Her khaki uniform bulged with the same virility that radiated from her shaven head.

"You should help the Pickens out, Mum. She been through very much with the husband."

"You know her? How did you—? No, no gift wrap," Donna Lee added as the cashier began to tie a bow around the festive paper he had wrapped the shade in.

"It comes with everything, Ma'am."

"Oh."

Donna Lee beamed warmly upon the cashier, just in case he was a Sanskrit scholar from Harvard.

Back in the cart the guard made another remark about helping the Pickens woman. As Donna Lee explained how busy she was, how she couldn't possibly find the time to take on another client, much less one who worked for that horrible Jesus spa, she felt her words undermined by an occasional glance from the guard. A strange sort of authority in those gray eyes made her excuses ring hollow.

"Just how do you know her, anyway?" Donna Lee said, interrupting her own protests to go on the offensive. "Do you realize what kind of woman she is? She goes to executioners' conventions and gets all sorts of kickbacks for that Jesus spa, I'm sure."

The cart slowed for a speed bump in the parking lot.

"She be my boss."

"Huh?"

"I work for the Pickens on Monday and Thursday. Over here rest of the week. In fact, you rude to me other day."

"What?"

"You on the phone screaming about balance for the kicksboxing."

"That was you? Well, I'm sure I wasn't screaming. My problem is really the opposite. I had to take a two-week seminar in assertiveness training last summer. Yes, it was that bad."

"This summer, Mrs. Keely, I suggest the anger management."


As she placed the lampshade in the backseat of her hybrid, Donna Lee continued to protest. "I don't really understand why that Pickens woman wants me to represent her. And by the way, I'm not 'Mrs.' Call me Donna Lee."

"You the best, that is why. No one can beat the whizzer."

Donna Lee didn't smile. "It's just a sideline, that's all."

The guard shook her round, shaven head, as neat as a melon. "No, Mum, you skin every cent from Mr. Travis Harper. Look at the ex now. She sit pretty in the pink mansion with the heated pool, the children, and ten thousands each month."

A curious mixture of pride and shame made Donna Lee deny any skill or accomplishment. At the same time, it bothered her that these facts and figures were being quoted by a security guard at the Tub-A-Rama.

"It is all public record," the guard said, as if reading her mind.

"I know, but still . . ."

"The Pickens, she look it up. When she see how well Mary Jo Harper do, she decide you the one for she."

"But I just can't work with that woman. It's impossible." She rooted in her backpack and brought out a business card. "Take this, will you? Give me a call. We have to talk. By the way, what's your name?"

The guard stared at the card a moment. "Iman. And Iman not getting a divorce."

"No, it's about something else, important. Or just drop by my office. It's right across the tracks from WaistWatch. Just make sure you don't tell Mrs. Pickens."

The cart's awning hid the guard's face again. "We will see, Mum." And she was off.

## The Camel's Yarn

One of the jets in the spa tub spurted so hard that water landed on the silk Covington rug that Mr. Van Buren had given Burma for their second wedding anniversary. This was another thing she had asked the caretaker to get fixed, the third jet from the left. Not only that, she nearly slipped and cracked her head open on the Teramo when she tried to get out of the tub.

"How many times do I have to ask before you do the simplest chore?" she called out, as she traipsed downstairs. For some reason there was a slight yodel in her voice. *Where in the hell did that come from?* she wondered.

A towel turbaning her head came unraveled as she tossed a bath grip at him. Vibrating in a red leather lounge chair, he didn't even bother to hold up his hands to catch it.

"Is it asking too much, Bobby? Especially after I went out and bought it myself?"

"You want me to screw a plastic handle in that priceless marble?"

"I told you to use Godzilla Glue."

He set the grip, which had landed in his lap, on a wobbly end table.

"No one's ever heard of Godzilla Glue. I asked every damn store in town."

"It's advertised in the *New Yorker,* Bobby. Just call them up, and don't put that glass on my good table."

She whisked away the pinot noir he was using to warm himself up and took a swig herself. Yes, an end table that had once belonged to Hugo Wolf, and he sets his glass down on it.

"Can't you put something on, Mrs. Van Buren?"

She cinched the Dolce & Gabbana minirobe a little tighter. It was not something she would ever wear at home, at her mother's, but it was the only thing she could find at the spur of the moment here. "I'm decent."

"What if someone saw you like that?"

"We're in the middle of nowhere, Miss Priss. Who's going to see me?"

Without budging from the chair, he parted a velvet drape. "The other day I could've sworn I saw Iman's Golf driving up."

"Look, Bobby, we're not doing anything wrong. I just come out here to give you a lesson."

After his impeachment, Mr. Pickens had developed a severe aversion to the Bible. Burma felt it part of her calling to set him straight. Once a week she planned to meet with her caretaker to discuss what Jesus really meant. This week they were doing the part about how tough it was to thread a needle with a camel.

"Mrs. Pickens told me that the Hebrew word for camel can also mean a coarse yarn," he had said before their inspection of the grounds. "She said this yarn could squeeze through a needle if it was greased just right."

But now after he had fallen through the ice, he didn't seem interested in her rebuttal. He just complained about his feet being cold.

"What's the point of saying it's hard for yarn to get through a needle?" she said after she had inserted Mr. Pickens's repulsive pink piggies into her late husband's slippers. Yes, she was glad she hated his neat, ladylike toes. It made it so much easier to resist pouncing on him and smothering him with kisses. Those lounging pajamas he had on, Mr. Van Buren's, made her so nostalgic for those long afternoons, hours and hours of bunnying . . .

"Would that make them want to crucify him?" she persisted. "Because of some greasy yarn? Don't you see, Bobby, Jesus really threatened the rich. He made them feel so uncomfortable."

"Burma, please, I've had enough for today. Go home."

"For your information, Mister, I am home."

"What?"

"This is my house, isn't it?"

"You're not planning on moving back in, are you?" He pulled a lever and sat upright. "You can't."

"And just why can't I?"

"You hate Elvis, remember?"

"Well, Mama's no picnic. She's really getting on my nerves."

"But she needs you, Burma. And besides, you're always preaching about the rich, how awful they are."

"I'm just as rich living at Mama's." With a sigh she collapsed onto a Méridienne. "And just as awful. Oh, Bobby, what's wrong with me? I want to do what Jesus says. I want to give it all away to the poor. But every time I try, someone stops me. Or it ends up in the wrong hands. And please don't floss in public."

The thread in his hand drooped.

"That's something you should do in private, Bobby, behind closed doors. Anyway, I thought I had the answer. That nonviolence foundation that wants to outlaw toy weapons for children. I was all set to fork over a bundle to them, Bobby, 'cause I really hate GI Joe and all that videogame crap. Then I got that call."

He swirled the pinot noir—three hundred a bottle Mr. Van Buren had paid—in his plastic cup. "What call?"

"You know, that anonymous call."

"Oh, the one that threatened to neuter Miss Brown?"

"No, not that one." She reached over and plucked the floss from the antimacassar on his chair. "Miss Brown's threat was about the money I gave to help defeat the gay marriage amendment."

"But you went ahead and gave, didn't you?"

"Well, I actually didn't want Miss Brown to have any puppies. It would've saved me a trip to the vet."

He sniffed the wine critically. "A lot of good your money did there, Burma. Fifty grand right down the drain."

She sighed. "I know, and Miss Brown's pregnant, too. If that guy calls again, I'm going to tell him thanks a lot. In fact, I should make him adopt the whole litter."

"You think it's the same guy calling about the nonviolent foundation?"

She shrugged. "Could be. Mama gets a lot of those calls herself.

She's always warning me about what might happen to Miss Brown and all. Anyway, I'm getting wore out by these threats, Bobby. It's really not good for Mama's nervous system. And she takes it all out on me. Just the other day she went ballistic over the check I wrote for the sodomites, as she calls them."

"Listen, I hate GI Joe, too, Burma. Just go ahead and give to that foundation. Don't let those creeps stop you."

Her eyes misted with a vague hope. "You do hate him?"

"Are you kidding? I used to get clobbered by this guy who had all the accessories. You ask me, this society is sick, truly sick, the way we encourage children to play at killing each other. It's the first thing most boys learn."

"Oh, Bobby, I never realized you felt this way."

"Little spinning wheels, that's what they should be playing with."

She idly wrapped his floss around her thumb. "No, those are just as bad, those little race cars. Makes them want to grow up and get in a horrible wreck for money."

"I'm talking about Gandhi."

"You mean those spindle things? Oh, Bobby, I can't believe my ears. I was feeling so alone, and now . . ." Her hand fluttered to his knee, which he didn't jerk away. At least, not at first.

"Easy there, Burma. You know my wife is fixing to sue me for every cent I got."

"But you don't got any, do you?"

"Well, there's the house. She's changed all the locks. And she's already started work on a guest bathroom she says I'm going to pay for. My Miata, too. She took that."

"Let her have that stupid car, Bobby. And that dumb ole house. I can fix you up with something much better. That hybrid Donna Lee drives. I could get you one of them."

"No sir, no way."

"What about one of them cute little Volkswagens, those Bunnies?"

"Listen, Burma, you're not getting me a Rabbit, hear?" He shook his head in a way that reminded her of that president who wasn't a crook, the one who threw up in China.

"Can you imagine what folks would say?"

"Who gives a flying fart, Bobby? Just suck it up."

"Suck what up? You want people to think I'm some sort of call boy? And do you realize that floss was in my mouth?"

Burma looked at the thread she had been using to dig out something trapped way back. "What did you say?"

"It's disgusting."

"Yes, sir, it sure is." She slapped her hand down so hard his cup toppled over. "If you think I'd pay one red cent to have sex with you, you're the biggest jerk this side of Liberty!"

"Thanks a lot," he muttered, dabbing at his wine-stained crotch.

"Did it ever occur to you that I might not have to pay for sex?"

"Now I'm going to have to change again."

"Take a good look at yourself, Bobby Pickens. Do you actually think any woman in her right mind would fork over a plug nickel to have that blubber of yours rubbing up against her, to see that jelly belly without a stitch covering it, naked, squirming nude against . . ."

"Down, boy."

The waxed thread dug into her thumbs, which had turned purple. "Why, I have a good mind now to give a fortune to that antitoy foundation, threat or no threat."

"Well, what's stopping you? You yap and yap about giving your money away. It's all talk. You're just as selfish as city hall, Burma, and you know it."

Tears welled up as she took a step or two away from the recliner. "Oh, Bobby, that's cruel."

Roused now by her retreat, he pointed an accusing finger at the mantel, where a photo of her late husband was decoupaged onto an urn shaped like a kneeling elephant.

"At least I never ran out and deliberately married one."

"Oh, Bobby, I didn't know. I really didn't. I just thought he was mean-spirited, that's all. I didn't realize he was an actual party member."

"Didn't know, huh? Well, what the hell else did you think someone like that would be?"

His conviction sent a chill of delight down her spine. "I was so young then, Bobby, so naive. Besides, you married one yourself, didn't you?"

"This isn't about me. It's about the way you let people walk all over you. First that husband of yours, and now that anonymous caller who won't let you give your money to a worthy cause. Don't be such a wimp, Burma. If you want to give to nonviolence, you give."

"But, Bobby, this threat was really scary."

"Hot air, that's all it is."

She dangled the thread over her bare thigh. "The man called at three A.M."

"So why do you pick up the phone at that hour?"

"I thought it might be Mama needing a glass of water. Anyway, when I pick up he says if I give that million to that commie Tolstoy Foundation, he's going to rip my balls off."

"What?"

"Well, not mine. Someone's."

"Someone's? What kind of threat is that?"

"Well, that wasn't the actual wording."

Unsashed, his smoking jacket open, he sat there with a bit of rosy flesh peeking through, looking so available.

"You don't have to be coy, Burma. He meant Dr. Schine, right?

That was the threat. You ask me, you got nothing to worry about. That guy looks like he can handle himself pretty well."

"Oh, he can, Bobby." She rearranged a fold of her minirobe so that it wasn't covering quite so much.

"In fact, it might not be a bad idea if he did get run out of town. That guy gives me the creeps."

"That's not very nice, Bobby."

"You realize how chummy he is with your mama? It's not right. He's up to something, better believe. Look how he wormed his way into Redds. I should be manager there, not him."

She gazed wistfully at him. "It'd be just like old times, Bobby, me and you doing inventory."

"What are you waiting for, then? Fire the man."

"I can't. Redds's fourteenth amendment says an assistant manager can't fire a manager, not even for gross malaise or something."

"Well, then, you give to the Tolstoy Foundation, hear? Send them a great big fat check."

"But Bobby—"

"You go, girl. Stop being such a coward. You want nonviolence in this world or not? Put your money where your mouth is."

"Oh, Bobby, you mean that?"

"I'm not just whistling Dixie."

She fiddled with the flap of his smoking jacket. "I always knew that underneath it all, real underneath, you were brave, Bobby. So big and brave."

"Yeah, well . . ."

Her hand crept beneath the flap. "And tall, too . . ."

"You must know, Burma, these macho guys, they're all show, no blow . . ."

"Don't I know, Bobby. Those little wienies wouldn't stand up to any threats, huh?" She was panting a little. "But you, you don't care if someone says he's going to neuter you. That's my man, all right."

"What? Me?" Mr. Pickens removed the hand from his crotch.

"Oh, Bobby, please," she urged, her hand at the flap again. "I'm so ready to give now. All you have to say is yes."

"I'm a registered Republican! Did you tell him that?"

"Right, Bobby, you're no girlie man. Just say yes, big boy, and I'll give . . ."

## The Foundation

*D*evotion. Donna Lee had never felt it before, at least as it applied to a human being. Her heart was given to the wetlands, to the vanishing coastline of Louisiana. It was a devotion that had launched a score of crusades over the years. She had battled the dragons belching pollutants from chemical plants and oil refineries all over southeast Louisiana. Jousting with infidel legislators she relished even more. But the beloved that had inspired her had been the storm petrel or night heron, creatures remote and wild, who really didn't give a damn about her. (Oh, how she adored their cool sufficiency, needing nothing at all from her.) She had never found anything worthy of true devotion in the male of her own species until a fifth Cosmopolitan.

Yes, that had been the turning point. They had eaten the duck, and it had been scrumptious. But one thing had been troubling her. He had said he was a guest in that house in Cherylview. Just whose house was it?

The answer was staring her in the face. In the dining room hung a gouache of a portly oilman, complete with derricks in the background. He sported a cowboy hat, chaps, and a six-shooter holster. The brass plaque beneath was engraved, "You Are My Sunschine."

"My brother," he said.

"You mean he moved down here, Dr. Schine? From Massachusetts?"

No, it was Dr. Schine who had moved away. He had been born down here—not in Tula Springs. Just a little farther out, fifteen miles. In Liberty.

Somehow, with his father raising hogs and soybeans, he had won a scholarship to Brown. Ever since, he had been scrutinizing his native land for some clue. To understand, after all, is to forgive. Yet the depth of Liberty's prejudice, the blind force of its fear and hatred of the poor threatened time and again to defeat his project. Louisiana's portable electric chair might no longer be trundling into Liberty, but the needle was still there, a savage vengeance that backed every official his brother voted for.

In a way, he was glossing her own story. Yet she didn't have anything so cut and dry to explain it all. She wasn't gay. O.K., being a woman was a start. But just look at all the ladies who were staunch supporters of their own oppression, not to mention that of the poor, as well. No, it was something else that connected her to his story.

It was that night, after the fifth Cosmopolitan that she had opened her purse. Out of it came the revolver, Mrs. LaSteele's.

He was right. We must disarm. It was the only way.

But he wouldn't take it from her. He wanted nothing to do with the circle of violence.

So she had put it back in her purse, where it still remained, a burden as awkward as the millions her client would like to give away.

. . .

"Whispering grass," he said when she asked about the sheave she had picked out.

"Is it natural?"

"Four ninety-nine," he said, not looking up from his computer screen.

*Well, excuse me, Mr. Manager of Redds Dipshit Emporium,* she would have said had she been in her right mind. No man had ever treated her this badly. *I'm so sorry to have intruded on your valuable time.*

"There's no one at the cash register, Dr. Schine. How do I pay for it?"

The door to the manager's office was ajar, but she was actually afraid to step inside.

The keyboard clicked officiously. "Just take it."

"I can't do that."

O.K., so he was gay. She had finally come around to accepting this, despite her initial doubts. That should have been the end of the story right there. But to her dismay she had discovered during the past four or five months, ever since first setting eyes on him, that she needed to be around him. In fact, she was teaching herself now that their relationship could be more intense, burn with a brighter flame, by not being consummated. Indeed, when she looked back at her entanglement with Mr. Harper, she felt a positive shame at her sordid lust. How glad she was that that was behind her. Now she could devote herself fully to something pure.

"By the way, do you think there's a vase these would look good in?"

He shrugged, still absorbed by the screen.

"I think I'll look around, if you don't mind. Oh, by the way, I want to thank you for that check."

He raised his glasses, those impossibly sexy glasses. Thin wires, tortoiseshell. "What check?"

"The Tolstoy Foundation."

Dr. Schine was handling Burma's finances now, not personally. But through his brother, he had found a reputable investment firm in Baton Rouge. Not long ago this would have thrown Donna Lee into a panic. She would have done everything possible to extricate her friend from this man's grasp. But at least his politics were sound. And just look what Mr. Harper had tried to do with Burma's estate. Had Burma donated Graceland II to AmStar, Donna Lee discovered that $750,000 would have been funneled to a PAC that financed election ads for judges who didn't believe in privacy. (Mr. Pickens had provided her with this information after his impeachment. So Dr. Schine, though she had been skeptical at first, had been telling her the truth at his duck dinner in Cherylview Estates.)

Could Dr. Schine's accountants in Baton Rouge be any worse than all this? Imagine Mr. Harper hiding that AmStar PAC from her, Donna Lee, when they were supposed to be so intimate! Burma was well out of that man's clutches.

"How did you know about that check, Keely?"

Donna Lee gave a little start. She had drifted back into the aisles to look for a vase and didn't realize the manager had left his office.

"I'm the one who asked Burma for a contribution. I'm on the board."

"Well, keep it quiet. Don't go yakking about it all over town."

His virile scent, almost a fragrance, invigorated her.

"I don't yak, Dr. Schine. Our newsletter will do a decent tribute to Burma."

"No way, Keely. This has to be anonymous."

"Look, Schine, I've had just about enough of your telling me what I can and cannot do. Why don't you get off that horse's ass and take a hike?"

The door chimes tinkled as a customer in a floor-length smock billowed not quite through the door. Donna Lee was there, too, trying to flee from the inane metaphors she had left in her wake.

A grunt, which at first Donna Lee thought was her own, actually came from the woman in the white muslin smock Donna Lee was attempting to squeeze past.

"Out of my face," the woman said, as Donna Lee's whispering grass brushed her nose. "I sneeze."

The chimes tinkled again as the two women struggled to dislodge themselves from the door. The turbaned woman was far more massive than Donna Lee had counted on. But Donna Lee's backpack was no help either.

"Now, Mum, you step back . . ."

Donna Lee knew that voice. Yet there was not enough distance to get a fix on what the woman actually looked like, especially with that turban.

"Mrs. Keely," the woman said, "please to step backward from Iman."

Yes, of course, the security guard. But she was dressed so differently. No more khaki uniform. And that turban she had on, it changed her altogether.

When she was finally able to turn, Donna Lee saw Dr. Schine smiling complacently at their simultaneous exit and entrance. Oh, that man, that horrible awful man!

# Enough Is Enough

*A*fter Iman had bought the plug-in scent she said she needed for the WaistWatch office, she followed Donna Lee up the stairs to the law office above Redds. Not in the least winded by the steep flight, the security guard paused in the doorway. Her brief survey took in the rusty Army-surplus file cabinets.

For a moment Donna Lee felt like a straight man subjected to the scrutiny of a queer eye. Every attempt she had made to brighten her drab surroundings seemed so pathetic now. Before she knew it she was apologizing for the duck on the A-C file cabinet, a gaudy duck that now looked vaguely obscene.

"Nothing here is mine, of course," she blathered. "Everything was given to me, little gifts, you know, from my clients." Including Mr. Harper. Oh, why hadn't she thrown that duck out? The man had no taste whatsoever.

Radiant in a white smock and turban, Iman seemed the only genuine article in the room. "What you need is a fern," she advised. "And some throws. The Pickens has an afghan that would do wonders for this baby." Her firm brown hand patted the tired sofa.

"Oh, no, don't, don't ask her."

"She need to get rid of office clutter, Mum. It will do the lady good."

With her finger the security guard wrote something on the grimy pane of a window looking out onto the railroad tracks. The angle of the sunlight, though, prevented Donna Lee from reading it. But she could see the town's new eyesore from this same window. A huge plasticine cross, twenty feet high, had gone up with WaistWatch emblazoned in neon across the top.

"Rather than the afghan, Iman, I'd like to see Mrs. Pickens get rid of that cross."

Donna Lee took a step or two toward the window, which she could now read. CLEAN ME.

"Wasn't the Pickens's idea."

"It's shocking, truly disgraceful. I'm sure it must be violating a building code." *Clean me?* How dare this woman write that on her window! "Did you people get a permit from the city?"

"Is this why you want to see Iman?"

She was perched on the sill, the duck in her hands. Donna Lee wished she would put the damn thing down. The leer in the duck's eye was unsettling.

"No. But anything you could do about that cross, Iman, I'd really appreciate. By the way, are you by any chance a Muslim?"

The woman's peerless complexion clouded over. "What you calling me that for, Mum?"

"Well, your name—and that turban."

"It be no turban. It be a wimple."

"Sorry, I just thought . . ." Donna Lee held up her hands, the way Dr. Schine did sometimes. "I didn't mean anything. Besides . . ."

"Besides what?"

*What's wrong with being a Muslim?* "Nothing. Oh, please, don't go. I'm really sorry."

The woman had left the sill and was drifting toward the door. "Well, just what do you want? The Pickens she is timing me, you know."

"Timing you?"

"Company policy. Employee must clock out during business hours."

"That's awful. I don't know how you put up with that, Iman. And why can't Mrs. Pickens get her own air freshener? Is that what you were hired for? To be her Steppin Fetchit?"

"Her what?"

Donna Lee had just assumed the woman was about as old as she was. But if she didn't get the reference . . . Yes, actually, Iman might be younger—even much younger. The heft was what made her seem more mature.

"How much is WaistWatch paying you, Iman?"

The woman's eyes narrowed. "That is pretty personal, Mum."

"Yes, it is."

"So why do you ask Iman that?"

"Because I guarantee if you come work for me, you'll do much better."

"You are not giving me a rib, no?"

"No, I need someone, Iman. A first-class assistant."

Business had been booming for Donna Lee recently. Especially after Mr. Harper's settlement, which had brought in a pretty penny. Word had spread about her ability as a divorce attorney, and she had far more cases than she could possibly handle, mostly because of an influx of wealthy evangelicals who had successfully lobbied to keep Adam from marrying Steve in Louisiana, God forbid.

"You won't have to work two jobs anymore. Just here with me."

"What the WaistWatch did with that cross," Iman said, her eyes narrowing as she turned away from the window. "It be very wrong." Taking a wooden crucifix from beneath her capacious muslin smock, she crossed herself. "Our Blessed Mother be very angry."

No other word needed to be spoken. Not even a mention of salary. She was aboard.

# The Tie That Binds

he Godzilla Glue came that morning by FedEx. Mr. Pickens had no choice now but to install the hand grip on the
spa tub. Defacing the Italian marble with a piece of plastic, well, it
didn't seem like something Burma should be in favor of. In any case,
if the grip weren't installed, Mr. Pickens wouldn't get reimbursed
for the cash he had shelled out to FedEx.

Which reminded him, he had to write down exactly how much he
had forked over this morning. Disgraceful that his own funds had to
be dispersed for this glue: $65.89. Why had the FedEx lady run off
without leaving a receipt? And why couldn't he find a scrap of paper
to write this down?

No, nothing in the King's playpen, not a scrap in the screening
room, the harem, or even the Mummy suite, where there was supposed to be a papyrus notepad. Upstairs, downstairs, and back up he
went looking for a simple piece of paper, interrupted twice by phone
calls, one from Burma's mother, who wanted to know if he'd seen her
good can opener. She'd looked everywhere in her own house, combed
every square inch including Burma's dresser, where she had discovered a perfectly good sweater set going to waste. The second call was
also from Mrs. LaSteele, who wanted to know why he had time to
gab about his boss's wardrobe when he should be installing that grip.
And by the way, she added, someone just called and said to tell you
you don't have long to bowl.

To bowl? I don't bowl.

You don't? Well, whatever, he said he's fixing to come get your balls.


He finally settled for a dried-out sheet of Biore facial wipe he came across in the powder room. Then, his mind clouded by this most recent threat, delivered courtesy of Mrs. LaSteele, he discovered that his pen holster wasn't loaded. Not a thing to write with.

What looked like a crayon on the windowsill turned out to be a lurid fake-looking insect. Shooing it out the window, Mr. Pickens noticed a man outside, way down by the end of the drive. Probably Dr. Schine. Well, this would be a good opportunity to speak to him about that glue. Maybe he could talk Burma out of ruining that good Italian marble. Of course, Mr. Pickens still expected to be reimbursed. In fact, maybe Dr. Schine had enough on him now to pay him back right away.

When Mr. Pickens got downstairs and opened the front door, he noticed the man was wielding a pick ax and tearing right into the Zen gravel by the highway.

"Sixty-five eighty-nine," Mr. Pickens reminded himself as he crunched past a granite boulder imported from Vermont.

"Sixty-nine eighty . . ." He pulled the Godzilla Glue from his pocket, ready to plead for the marble's life. See, he did care about the environment. What if this awful glue seeped into the spa tub while he was whirlpooling?

As he neared the highway, he saw the man had cast aside the pick. He was now setting something into the hole he'd made. A birch? Yes, it was white as a birch, but there was something artificial about it.

Pausing by another boulder, Mr. Pickens squinted toward the rising sun. No, it wasn't a tree at all. It was a cross, a large white cross. And there was something odd about this guy. He seemed too slight to be Dr. Schine, less substantial.

The cross sank into place, upright now.

Mr. Pickens crouched behind the boulder and peered around. On the gravel next to the cross was a robe, like something a priest might wear. Oh Lord Almighty, it must be the Klan! Of course, they were the ones after his bowling balls. How Burma could have contributed to the Tolstoy Foundation knowing that he'd be in mortal danger—well, it was criminal. A hundred thousand for nonviolence? No, sir, it was a hundred grand aimed right at his innocent, unadulterated manhood!

His heart thumping, Mr. Pickens picked out 911 on his cell.

Busy.

A chameleon sunning itself on the mica-encrusted granite blinked as Mr. Pickens duck-walked back toward the house.

Busy again.

Luckily, he made it inside without the derobed Klansman spotting him. And he'd had a chance to secure the outside doorknob.

Mr. Pickens tried the number again.

"Good morning, AAA SecureCarc. This month we have a special on Orange Alert DayGlo—"

"Yes, yes, I know," Mr. Pickens said. "Please send a car out to Graceland as soon as possible."

"Have you heard about our new carbon monoxide monitor? Let us install one in the comfort of your home and—"

"Look, it's me, Carl Robert Pickens. Who's this?"

"We're sorry. We're not at liberty to divulge our human resource database. Press the pound key for any—"

"Oh, just shut up and listen, Edsell."

It was his administrative assistant from city hall—or rather, former assistant. The nerve of Edsell to have inserted himself into the security agency after he, Mr. Pickens, had been impeached.

"Edsell, this is extremely important. Tell the dispatcher to send an armed car out to Graceland in a jiffy."

"We are the dispatcher."

"All right, then. Send one out."

"What seems to be the problem, Brother Bobby?"

"A five-oh-one is in progress."

Static clogged the cell for a moment or two. "Copy. Aggravation in progress, sexual aggravation."

Mr. Pickens sighed. "Edsell, five-oh-one is assault, sexual assault. And furthermore . . ."

The door chimes rang.

Mr. Pickens whispered into the cell, "He's at the door. What should I do?"

"It's me, Brother Bobby. Let me in."

Of course, this made perfect sense. Edsell had been out to get him from day one. And with all that praying in public, he was bound to join the fold and don the sheet's clothing.

"Come on now, open up!"

Like the wisest of the three pigs, Mr. Pickens felt rather secure in his brick house. Especially when the knob of the locked door began to rattle furiously.

## A Summons for Burma

"*F*ive point six million?"

Burma wiped away a tear as she handed over the summons she had just been served by their waitperson. "I hope you're satisfied."

"Me?"

"You're the one made me come here."

Burma had wanted to celebrate at Dick's China Nights, where the Tuesday night all-you-can-eat buffet was only $7.95. Instead, Donna Lee had insisted on Isola Bella, the home of the $7.95 scallop. Yes, that was her appetizer, one measly scallop lurking beneath a raw quail egg.

"Quiet," Donna Lee said as Burma complained of a draft rattling the window next to them. "Let me read."

Burma stuffed a linen napkin into the noisy, unpainted sash. It used to be one of the plainest homes in Tula Springs, this restaurant. When she was a girl, Burma had felt sorry for the family that had to live here, right across the street from the beauty college where her mother had taught beehives. Somehow the homely wood-frame house had become the chicest place in town. Donna Lee had explained how the chipped paint on Burma's chair bottom was all part of the same distress that made the crack in her salad plate so right.

Glass squeaked as Burma subtracted 5.6 from 37 on a humid windowpane. Thanks to the investment firm in Baton Rouge that Dr. Schine had recommended, her net worth had soared in the past two months. It made her so nervous, too, getting richer and richer without lifting a finger. And now this summons.

A chorus of waitstaff suddenly loomed, singing "Happy Birthday" with the menacing tone used by people with better things to do.

Burma wiped out the figures on the cracked pane as something was set on fire in front of her. Cherries jubilee.

"Who is this Morone anyway?" Donna Lee demanded as the final "You" of the copyrighted song faded away.

"How can you ask me who he is?" Burma said. "He's the guy who flosses you. Don't you even know his name, girl?"

"Lord. Mr. Pickens's assistant, right?"

"Former assistant."

The waitperson who had served her the summons asked if there'd be anything else.

Blowing out the dessert prevented Burma from delivering a stinging riposte. He was gone before she recovered her breath.

"I'm not letting you pay for this, Donna Lee. I'm sure anything on fire must cost at least fifteen bucks."

"Would you stop harping on how much everything costs?" the attorney said, still frowning at the summons. "Chill out. Enjoy."

"Now the whole world knows it's my birthday. Great."

There was something shameful about turning sixty-two with no man at your table. How she had pleaded with Mr. Pickens to join them. But even though he was tempted by a free meal at the town's best restaurant, in the end he was too concerned about being neutralized. So he stayed locked up securely in Graceland. As for Dr. Schine, he had flown back to Massachusetts to celebrate his wedding anniversary.

"So then Mr. Pickens thought the Klan was after him," Burma was saying a few minutes later, after Donna Lee had gone to the restroom to check on Mrs. LaSteele. It seemed that Burma's mother wasn't having gastric problems. She was just helping her niece, the restroom matron, fold towelettes.

"That's why he called 911. Because he saw that cross and the white thing that looked like a robe but was only a tarp."

"Hold on," Donna Lee said. "It was Edsell who answered the 911 call?"

Burma took a sip of the Tuscan dessert wine Donna Lee had ordered for them both. Twelve dollars a glass, and the girl hadn't one decent blouse in her wardrobe.

"Well, see, after Mr. Pickens was fired from SecureCare for moral turpitude, it made sense that Edsell would take over that job, too, I guess."

"Moral turpitude?"

"That's what they called getting impeached. They don't want anyone impeached working at SecureCare."

The day after the impeachment the mayor had appointed Mr. Pickens's administrative assistant interim superintendent of Streets, Parks, and Garbage. It was temporary, of course, until the city could raise enough money to hold another election.

"So when Edsell went to see what was wrong in the house, Mr. Pickens thought it was a Klansman coming after him, the one who planted the cross on the lawn. That's why Mr. Pickens covered the doorknob with Godzilla Glue before locking himself inside. He wanted the Klansman to stick to the knob until help arrived. Only Edsell didn't stick. He pulled away O.K. It was when he was trying to wash the stuff off his hands in the catfish pond. That's when he slipped into the pond and swallowed all the microbes in the summons. His doctor says he's sick for life. This amoeba has set up shop in his intestines and won't leave for nothing because of the raw sewage in the pond."

A grim smile played upon Donna Lee's face. "Planting a cross on your property, huh? Well, we'll just see if they get a penny out of you, girl. In fact, we're going to countersue first thing tomorrow morning. Defacing your property. Terrorizing your handyman. Extortion, threats . . . We'll crack this Klan right open. I'll have the names of every member in this administration. Yes, Ma'am, this burg is headed for a makeover. After I get through, there won't be a single recognizable face in city hall."

She reached across the table for a taste of Burma's jubilee. "What surprises me is how stupid they are, doing it in broad daylight. But I guess you never can underestimate—what is it?"

Something sticky and hard in the dessert had kept Burma from correcting her attorney right away. She was waving her hand instead.

"Well, actually," Burma ventured once her tongue had cleared away the pit, "I gave Edsell the cross."

"You did? Why?"

"For the grounds."

"Burma, you mean you actually wanted it there? A twelve-foot cross on your property?"

"What's wrong with that? In case you forgot, I *am* a Christian."

"You scared the living shit out of Pickens, girl. That's what's wrong."

"It's just plastic, Donna Lee, from WalMark. Real lightweight, hollow, and easy to assemble. If Bobby had any sense, he could've seen it'd never burn."

"How could he see clear to the end of your drive? So now you got yourself a huge lawsuit. Are you happy?"

Burma did not like this tone of voice. "I won't discuss it anymore. Not tonight."

"But why did you do something so . . . ?"

"So what? Dumb? Stupid?"

Donna Lee shrugged. "Let's say inconsiderate."

"I was going to tell Bobby all about it. But Edsell got there sooner than I expected. He said he'd do it after work, when I got home from the store."

"What were you doing talking to Edsell anyway? This just doesn't make any sense. You know that he's already made a shitload of trouble for Pickens. Why would you—"

"Stop, just stop." Burma dabbed at her eyes and blew her nose. "Look, it's my birthday. I'm determined to have a good time, hear?" She held up her glass as her waitperson passed by. "More wine please, you asshole."

# The Night Heron

*W*ith Dr. Schine away in Massachusetts, Donna Lee could hardly get through the day. The Mexican plum in front of her apartment looked as dull as the hornwood in the vacant lot behind Redds. A garter snake, lured into the open by an unusually muggy January afternoon, turned, upon closer inspection, into a shriveled piece of rubber.

But then one day there he was, opening the door to the feed and seed that was going out of business again. Her heart swelled painfully.

He hadn't let her know he was back. Just her floor, his ceiling, separated them at work. Yet he hadn't bothered to pick up the phone, much less climb the stairs, with a little keepsake from Massachusetts. Yes, she had been imagining how sweet it would be if he would bring her a jar of blueberry preserves his husband had put up.

Without even glancing at the feed and seed's plate-glass window, she strolled by casually. She'd be damned if she would go inside. If he was too high and mighty to call her, to give her a simple hello, well then, she wasn't going to throw herself at his feet. Even if they did have so many important matters to discuss, business matters, why should she be the one initiating the discussion? Sure, Burma's cross needed immediate attention, but he was bound to misinterpret her overture. He would think she was desperate for his friendship. He might even think she was still hoping he might not be gay underneath it all. That somehow she might get through to him in a way no other woman possibly could. Well, she'd be damned if she would encourage such nonsense. Long ago she had accepted that he was 100 percent queer. Yes, he could be the very first man she had loved simply for being himself, not for any ulterior motive about satisfying any need of her own. But if he chose to ignore this totally pure disinterested friendship she offered . . .

Halfway down the block she turned around and headed back to the feed and seed. Oh, what luck! He was backing out of the door now with a huge bag in his arms.

"Careful, Auntie," he said, as he peered out from behind the bag of mulch. They had nearly collided, accidentally, of course.

Oh, it wasn't Dr. Schine at all. It was some hick with a red face, a flat nose. What was her problem? Yes, he did have a similar build—and that luscious black hair did look so much like his. But this face, so round, was nothing like his chiseled perfection.

A piercing horn stopped her dead in her tracks. So anxious to get away from that man, she had walked right into Flat Avenue without looking either way.

"You trying to get killed?"

Be my guest, Mr. Fat Hog Lexus. Run right over me. I've had enough. *Auntie!* How dare that clodhopper call her that!

She was on the other side of Flat headed for her office when the Lexus pulled over.

"You O.K.?" she heard as the tinted window descended.

It was Mr. Harper, the last person in the world she wanted to see.

"Just fine," she said, without breaking stride.

The SUV continued to trail her down the block.

"Would you stop for a minute, Donna Lee?"

"Go away."

He pulled to the curb, and after taking up two handicapped spaces, swung the door open.

Hot shame made her almost run toward Redds. Knowing Dr. Schine now, Donna Lee found it hard to believe that she had once tangled with this man in bed, her own bed. Oh, and not just once. Time and again. What had she been thinking? Did she ever believe he could be redeemed? No, deep down she had always known he was nothing but a fascist, and no amount of loving was going to change that awful truth.

"Slow down."

"Go away, Travis."

"Please, just a minute. Give me a minute."

She was halfway up the stairs to her office when she turned, exhausted.

"Leave me alone, please."

"I need to talk to you." His face looked gray, drained of that glow that had made him so appealing in the old days, before Schine. "Business."

With a sigh, she turned and climbed the remaining stairs to her office. An ache in her knee made her ascent a little lopsided.

"Well, what is it?"

Though he had platinum memberships in three health clubs, he was too winded to answer. This made her knee feel better.

"Travis, I'm very busy. I don't have time to . . ."

"That lawsuit," he managed to get out.

"Which one?"

"Edsell's." He perched on the edge of her desk. "I was just wondering if you were going to be representing Burma."

"What business is it of yours?"

"Well, since I'm representing Edsell, I thought it would be better if you weren't involved."

"You? You're just an accountant."

"With a law degree."

She wished he'd get off her desk. He was crushing an important deposition. "You're kidding."

"I passed the bar."

"Then what made you become an accountant?"

"I discovered I couldn't stand lawyers."

She stared blankly at him. With the new lampshade installed, the light in the office was less harsh, more flattering. She would need the old fluorescent tube, though, to read his face properly.

"You actually are going to represent that idiot?" she finally said. "Good luck."

"The superintendent of Streets, Parks, and Garbage happens to have a serious disability, Ms. Keely. The pond water was so polluted by leaking sewage that the amoeba might never be eradicated. Burma is obviously responsible for the damages incurred by the willful mischief of her employee."

"Come on, Harper. Five point six million for a little Godzilla Glue? You don't stand a chance."

She yanked the deposition from under his fanny. "Right here, I've got sworn testimony from a senator who got stuck to a toilet seat in a casino restroom. With the exact same glue. And he's doing just fine, thank you, a model inmate."

A prolonged screech, like a monstrous Band-Aid being ripped from an open wound, made Travis's hand, which had strayed to her firm kickboxer's butt, yank back.

"What the hell?"

"Keep that door shut," Donna Lee said, as he peered into the hallway. "It's just Iman. She's remodeling the washroom. It's going to be her office."

"WaistWatch is moving over here?" he asked, as a mushroom cloud of dust blossomed in the hall. A white gauze mask covering her nose and mouth, Iman dragged a heating duct, thick as an anaconda, past the gaping neo-attorney.

"Shut that door!" Donna Lee snapped, noticing for the first time how thin the hair was on the back of his head. And did he seem much wider in the rear?

Slapping the plaster dust that had settled onto her sofa, Donna Lee answered when he asked a second time. The door was shut now. "No, WaistWatch is not moving here. Iman is. She's my new assistant."

"You hired a Republican?"

"Yes, sir, I did. A Republican who's sick to death of your hypocrisy. It was the cross that did it. That cross those idiots put up in front of WaistWatch."

Mr. Harper fondled his plastic duck as she yanked open the Venetian blinds. Across the railroad tracks the twenty-foot cross had "WaistWatch" emblazoned where "INRI" should have been.

"Might I remind you, Ms. Keely, that I have nothing to do with WaistWatch. Besides, your client has put up a cross of her own."

The way he stroked the duck, those beautiful fingers of his, which could play her flesh as miraculously as Murray Perahia's unraveling a knotty Bach fugue, it made her ache so badly for Dr. Schine. A simple phone call from him would have given her so much strength. Just the most mundane call.

"That's different. Iman can understand Burma's cross."

A devout Catholic, Iman might well be able to. But Donna Lee was still having a hard time fathoming Burma's real intent. Plied with another glass of dessert wine at her birthday dinner, Burma had reverted to the topic she had closed. She was going to make peace with the anonymous caller by demonstrating how much everyone had in common. After all, she was just as much a Christian as the number-one suspect was. (Edsell, Burma was sure, had to be the caller who was making all those threats.) If he could only get that through his thick skull, maybe Mr. Pickens would be left in peace to enjoy his upcoming divorce.

"But everyone knows Burma is against the war," Mr. Harper said.

"And she doesn't believe in capital punishment. What the hell is she doing putting up a cross?"

"It was your client who put it up, Harper. Edsell himself."

"Yes, because he thought Burma had finally repented of her sick humanism."

"And become prowar and prodeath, right? No, Harper, don't . . . I can't. Iman is right outside and . . ."

"Ms. Keely, please, dear bug . . ."

"Oh, stop, you've got to stop . . ."

"I miss you so much. I'm all alone now."

"I know it's not easy, but I can't . . . Really."

"You're not suing me anymore, remember? You've already screwed me royally in court, babe. This will be very ethical, our first ethical—"

"No, I can't . . . Oh, you poor wretch . . . Is that a tear?"

"Hold me, that's all. Just hold me. Nothing else."

"That's it, Harper. I'll hold you, but no more . . . Nothing else."

"How can you have a Christian society, Donna Lee, without making people pay for their sins? It's just not possible. There wouldn't be any law at all then."

Donna Lee snatched the Bible on her desk and shook it in his face. "You're right, Travis. That's exactly what Galatians is all about, the abolition of the law. It's liberation from male and female, slave and free, Gentile and Jew. In Christ all this is abolished."

Still semierect because of the Viagra spammed to him, Mr. Harper smiled up at her. "This is great. Here you are preaching to me. I never thought I'd see the day."

"Look, I used to believe just like you and Edsell do, Travis."

"How so?"

"I believed that Christianity was a culture of death and oppression, of the worst sexism imaginable. But when Burma started talking about Galatians the other night, something dawned on me. No, don't smile. This is serious. Law, the literal reading of any text, this kills as surely as the electric chair at Angola."

With a tissue, he wiped himself off. "Lethal injection, darling. Those scum die a much less painful death than most of us ever will."

"Nice. Did Jesus call the thief he was dying with scum? The soldiers who tortured Jesus before he was legally put to death by the state, they used that word, Travis, don't you think?"

"He's a dangerous dude."

"Who?"

"That Dr. Schine. Somehow he's gotten to you, too. Not just Burma."

"What are you talking about? This has nothing to do with him."

"He's going to bilk every last cent out of her."

"Get over it. So he took away her account from you. You have plenty of other clients."

Propping himself on an elbow, a naked thigh exposed, he morphed into Angela Lansbury's pose in the Samson flick that had put Donna Lee to sleep the other night.

"Just what do you know about that man?" he asked.

"That investment firm in Baton Rouge has outperformed you, Travis. It's made Burma a shitload. And you were going to sell her out for that stupid PAC."

"I'm asking about him. What do you know, Donna Lee? Anything at all?"

Buttoning her work shirt, Donna Lee didn't answer. But when he repeated the question yet again, she put into words something she didn't realize until that very moment.

"What do I know? Last night I was taking out the garbage. When

I got downstairs and headed toward the bins behind the building, my heart went wild, a full-blown anxiety attack. I didn't see it at first. But it saw me. I had only a glimpse, and then it was gone."

His eyebrows raised a notch. "What was it?"

"Something so wild, Travis. I never felt such joy."


## Manning the Barricades


In order to protect Mr. Pickens from an upsurge of anonymous threats, Burma had packed a few essentials into an overnight bag and moved into Graceland II. A temporary arrangement, of course, until things settled down. Burma's letter to the *Herald*, explaining that her cross meant Graceland was a Death-Free Zone, had enraged the anonymous caller. He really didn't sound much like Edsell, after all, not when Burma pressed her ear real hard against the receiver. Her stance against the death penalty and the war made Mr. Pickens, the caller said, a traitor as well as an atheist. "And you know, Miss, what traitors deserve. Look it up in your Bible."

As if this weren't bad enough, Iman had written her own letter to the *Herald* to explain the cross at Graceland. It was planted there to remind every citizen of Tula Springs that any form of birth control was condemned by God. Walgreen's better look out, Iman wrote. Not just the morning-after pills, but any pill or condom or gel would not be tolerated in Tula Springs. This included the rhythm method, a prohibition she would personally enforce.

"What's the rhythm method?" Mr. Pickens asked, as he perused the morning paper that contained this letter.

151

"Something the Catholics do, like having your cake and eating it."

"You say here it's 'the sneakiest, most hypocritical way of having sex just for pleasure.'"

"That's not me, Bobby. That's Iman. I swear that woman has some gall signing my name to her letter."

"'Using nature itself to subvert nature,'" he continued to read. "'It's a hundred times more diabolical than a condom, which is at least honest in its intent to subvert God's plan for procreation.'" He slapped the page. "I still have no idea what the rhythm method is. You sure you didn't write this letter? 'Cause it sure doesn't sound like Iman."

"Of course I didn't. Just let it go, Bobby. It has nothing to do with you."

"My ass it doesn't. You realize I got a nasty call from the rectory at Our Lady this morning? Six A.M., and I have to listen to some priest chew me out, saying how moral the rhythm method is, approved by all the church fathers and the current pope for hundreds of centuries. I swear, Burma, I could barely get back to sleep."

"Look, I done told you that wasn't my letter. The *Herald* should never have printed it with my name. I swear, the media's getting about as sloppy as you, leaving your underpants right by the fridge. Why do I have to come down for prune juice first thing in the morning and get turned on? Can't I get some peace in this house?"

He munched his oats thoughtfully.

"You're going to write a rebuttal, right, Burma? You're going to tell them it wasn't you."

"Nothing I say now is going to help. Besides, what do I care about birth control?" She gave him a hard look. Like the current pope, Burma had few worries about getting pregnant. If Iman wanted the cross to stand for that, too, then that was fine with her. Just fine and dandy.

"That's not why you're getting those threats anyway, Bobby. The capital punishment stuff is what tees the caller off."

"And you make me eat oatmeal."

"Pardon?"

"Why should I worry about cholesterol when he's fixing to neuter me. The least I might get out of it is sausage, real sausage."

"Pass the yogurt."

"But it's not fair. I believe in capital punishment."

Burma was hoping she hadn't heard right. "Would you *please* pass the yogurt? How many times must I ask?"

He shoved it across the table. They were in Graceland's breakfast nook. Movie posters from *Girls! Girls! Girls!* surrounded the dinette booth that had actually been used in the film.

"So what rhythm do they use, the Catholics? Is it something different from in and out?"

"No, it's where the man pulls out at the very last minute, something I really do disapprove of. The sin of Omar, that's what Mama's preacher calls it. And just what the hell do you mean by saying you believe in capital punishment? Do you think I put that cross up there to celebrate death, Bobby Pickens?"

"Oh, brother. Here we go."

"Well? Do you think the state was right to execute God himself? It was all legal, you know."

"O.K., I agree as far as God goes. But, Lord, Burma, what about the goons who commit those horrible crimes?"

"I'll tell you what. They're all poor, that's what. And they all live here in the South, which accounts for more executions of black men—innocent and guilty alike—than the rest of the country combined. It's lynching all over again, Bobby. Another form of lynching."

Enlightening him drained so much energy that she forgot the most important item on the breakfast agenda. He had two court appearances on Wednesday at 10:30 A.M.: one in Room 39 for his divorce and the other in Room 112 for Edsell's civil suit against her. When she remembered, she was already at Redds, setting out a display of drain guards.


"No problem," he said that evening, when she brought up the scheduling conflict.

It had been such a long, weary day for her. Without Dr. Schine, who was still in Massachusetts, Redds hung like a millstone around her neck. Every minute, though vapid and empty, went over like a bad joke's balloon.

"Just let him chop me up like he threatens to, Burma. Then I can be in both courtrooms."

"That's defeatest talk, Bobby. I don't want to hear defeatest talk."

They were sipping apple martinis out on the north balcony. In the past couple of weeks they had discovered that this balcony, adjoining the master bathroom, was the most comfortable in winter. Here the light didn't slant into their eyes. Yet there was more warmth than any of the other balconies afforded. Also, it was so easy to take a leak. Both Burma and Mr. Pickens suffered from overactive bladders, which even prescription pills couldn't staunch.

"Don't you realize we live in a great nation, Bobby? It's near perfect. I can't imagine any other nation on earth where we could be living like this." She gestured vaguely at a far-flung catfish pond, which reflected the lurid pink sunset in more muted, suitable glory.

"Here I'm about to be sued out both ends at once," Mr. Pickens mused, "not to mention lynched, and you sit there spouting red, white, and blue."

With a blank expression on her rosy, unlined face, she freshened her martini. Why she had said those things to him, she wasn't sure.

Just before closing time at Redds that afternoon, a certain customer had spouted this same spiel to her after she, Burma, had refused to ring up a boxed set of Clint Eastwood DVDs. It was nice for once, Burma supposed, not to be on the receiving end of that speech.

"Just stop talking so defeatist," Burma said, the martini shaker still in her hand. "There's a simple solution. All you got to do is call Donna Lee up and tell her to change one of the hearings."

"Which Donna Lee am I calling?" he said after a brief sulk. A silver bell's branch shivered a few notes onto the pond. "Which one, Burma? My defense attorney in Edsell's suit, or the Donna Lee who's suing me in divorce court?"

"Just call her. And stop making such a big deal that she's representing your wife, too."

No matter how many times she explained, he just couldn't seem to get it into his head: Donna Lee had decided to represent Mrs. Pickens in the divorce suit for his own good. For one thing, Donna Lee would make sure the woman didn't get anything but the bare minimum out of his hide. Furthermore, this would give Donna Lee an opportunity to investigate WaistWatch. She was convinced that something fishy was going on at that spa, that money was being laundered from tax-exempt faith-based initiative funds into the mayor's reelection purse.

"Well, it just doesn't feel right, Burma, being sued and defended by the same woman on the same day at the same exact time."

"Get over it. Just focus on how pretty that pond looks, all pink like that."

While his eyes were on the pink, she topped off his martini.

# What Next

"Shouldn't you be over at the courthouse, Daughter?" Mrs. LaSteele asked.

"Now I lost count."

Burma was trying to figure out how many Tolstoy Foundation DVDs she had given away that week.

"I'm going to have to start all over again."

"I suppose you don't mind losing six million to that knucklehead."

"Mama, it's the divorce now, Mr. Pickens's divorce. My trial isn't till next week. And besides, it's only five."

A significant look from Mrs. LaSteele made Burma lose count again. They had had another argument that morning about Burma sleeping over at Graceland. Mrs. LaSteele was sure her daughter's name would be dragged through the mud during the divorce proceedings. Burma said she didn't care what people thought about her and Mr. Pickens. Much to her regret, there was absolutely no mud to be dragged through. They were still pure as the driven snow—even after she'd tried her best to get him drunk on those apple martinis.

"You sure it's only five million? I thought it was six point something."

"Now you made me lose count again! Go away, Mama."

With a sniff, Mrs. LaSteele attended to the customer who had just walked in.

"Aisle five," Burma heard her mother say.

When the customer returned to the counter with a bathroom cleanser, Burma asked her if she had ever considered pumice.

Burma set the customer's bottle behind the counter and brought out one of the pumice stones she kept handy. With that great big fat wedding ring on her finger, the woman looked as if she could afford a little ecological sanity.

"That'll be $25.96."

"What? Where is my Tidy Bowl?"

"Ma'am, this pumice won't pollute our ponds and rivers. And you get a free DVD with it, a twenty-nine ninety-five value."

The woman peered at the drawing on the Tolstoy Foundation's retelling of *Snow White*. "A spinning wheel? What's that supposed to mean?"

"Soft on crime, that's what," Mrs. LaSteele put in.

"Mama, you keep out of this."

"A hundred grand she doles out for these fairies' tales," Mrs. LaSteele said, waving the DVD she had snatched away from the customer. "And her own mother can't purchase a box set of real American beef, Mr. Clint Eastwood. Why, there won't be one cent left for my old age. These soyheads will bleed her dry. I ask you, can you imagine such an ingrate?"

This appeal was made to Iman, not the customer, who had fled the store with neither pumice nor chemicals.

Iman shrugged. She had stopped by Redds for some mousetraps. Her office upstairs, she explained to Mrs. LaSteele, was plagued by little scritchy sounds that made it hard to proofread the depositions for Mr. Pickens's divorce proceedings.

"Don't I know," Mrs. LaSteele commented, as Iman examined a deluxe trap.

"Don't you know what, Mama?" Burma couldn't help saying. "You've never proofread a thing in your entire life."

Mrs. LaSteele sniffed again. "For your information, Daughter, it was me caught the mistake."

"What mistake?"

"Your name. Your daddy and me named you 'Bertha' after that big gun. That's what a blast you give us, such a shock. I thought I was just putting on a little weight since your daddy swore up and down he never fucked without a sheepskin."

"Mama!" Burma smiled apologetically at Iman, whose face was as stony as Easter Island. "'Bertha,' Mama? Just what are you telling me?"

"That's what me and Daddy wanted to call you. But my mama, you know how she always had to have her way—well, sir, she filled in the name *she* wanted. Burma. That was her cat's name, and I wasn't about to have no daughter named after no cat. But then your daddy being real devout and all, he says once something's written down, it's like scripture. That's it, baby. You don't mess with scripture."

Shaking her head, Iman handed Burma a five for the mousetraps. As Burma made change, she said, "I just hope you're satisfied, Mama. Is it any wonder I'm still unmarried after all these years? What man would ask out someone who sounds like a can of shaving cream?"

"Darling girl, Burma just happens to be the name of one of the loveliest places on earth." Mrs. LaSteele pulled out a chopstick from her bun and rapped the counter with it. "Your name's about as romantic as you can get."

"Actually," Iman said, as she pocketed her change, "it not called that anymore, Mrs. It be one of the worst regimes ever, almost as bad as that word you use. But still we must thank the Lord that Mr. Daddy don't use sheepskin, no?"

"No," Mrs. LaSteele said, as her daughter, clutching her satchel, followed Iman out the door with profuse apologies.

"Where you going, daughter?"

"Just upstairs for a minute, Mama. If that lady comes back, don't you dare give her that Tidy Bowl, hear? I'll tell Dr. Schine on you, better believe."

Burma gently eased the office-warming gift out of her Fendi satchel. How nice it looked when she set it on Iman's desk. The embedded Amazonian butterfly had been rejected by Mrs. LaSteele as a Mother's Day gift years ago. A brilliant turquoise, the insect added just the right touch to the room. Yes, Iman had done wonders with the space. The ovoid desk on which a modest carved snake writhed beneath the feet of a teak Queen of Heaven gave the snug room a certain character. Compared to this, Donna Lee's office was a long, drawn-out yawn.

"Yes, is very nice," Iman said about the butterfly after some prompting.

Burma could barely see the crack in the plasticene that framed the butterfly, a hairline crack that only a mother could notice.

"To me it symbolizes the rain forests that BurgerMat is destroying," Burma went on.

"Woman, what you want?" A gold lorgnette was raised from Iman's imperial bosom. "You want for the jungle to take over so we go back to savage pagans who use the four-letter word?"

With a pleasant smile, Burma pretended not to mind being peered at like she was some sort of grand opera, complete with camels, slaves, and loony mothers. "Not exactly."

"You like dysentery and fish what eat men?"

"I can't rightly say I'm fond of them."

"Then as you see, Mum, I be extremely busy." The lorgnette dropped back onto its chain. "I still have to testify at the Pickens's

trial myself this afternoon, and Mrs. Keely, she want for me to orga-
nize the depositions . . . Hear that? Scritchy scratch?"

Burma put her ear to the wall. Yes, there was definitely something
back there. She told Iman she would get her some more traps, free.

"Free? No, Mum, we take nothing free. Not in this office. The
Pickens told me you might try funny business."

"Oh, they're just sample traps, Iman, floor models we get for
free." Burma coughed. She had to come to the point. It was now or
never. "In any case, I was just wondering if you really had to bring up
that bush this afternoon."

"What bush?"

"The sweet olive. I really don't think it's right to humiliate Mr.
Pickens in court like that. He didn't do nothing but answer the call of
nature, I swear, that's all it was."

Iman's satiny arms were folded across the lorgnette. "Is that all?"

"No, it isn't all. As a matter of fact, I think it's so unfair that Mrs.
Pickens is saying she can't be married to a racist."

"It's on tape, Mum. He say it himself, that he hates the colored
African American."

"As a joke, that's all. And besides, you're not even African American, are you? Why should you care about that?"

The other day Donna Lee had told Burma another reason Iman
had quit working at WaistWatch, besides the blasphemous cross.
Iman was sick and tired of Mrs. Pickens referring to her as an
African American when she had told her, time and again, that she
was a Carib from Grenada.

"I swear that man is about the least racist person I've met in my
entire life," Burma went on, avoiding the implacable gaze of the dark
teak queen. "He's literally color blind, you know, always wearing a
black sock with a navy. I just wish you'd give him a break, Iman,
and—what? Don't you like it?"

Iman was holding out the framed butterfly. "We can't, Mum."

"Can't what?"

"Take no bribe. As a fact, I should be telling the Judge Brown you tamper with the witness."

The butterfly seemed curiously heavy in Burma's hands. She gazed at it sadly. "I feel very sorry for you, Iman. An innocent gift of friendship and office warming, you turn into something suspect."

"Good day, Mum."

Dumping the turquoise beauty into her Fendi, Burma rallied her pride. "All right, if you're giving back bribes, how about that five hundred I gave you?"

"So you admit it be a bribe, Mum? To keep me from talking about you and the awful lecher man."

"What? No, I don't admit nothing, especially that he's a lecher man."

"In that case, Mum, we don't worry about bribes. Sioux City I did not enjoy as anticipated. It rains the whole time I be there."

## Don't Ask

*A*t Bible study later that week Burma interrupted Donna Lee's analysis of *arsenokoetis* to ask about the terms of Mr. Pickens's divorce. Would he be able to keep his own house on Sweetgum?

". . . commonly referring to male temple prostitutes rather than homosexuals, a term that simply didn't exist until the late nineteenth century. So you see—Burma, quit waving your hand, please."

"I asked a question."

161

"It's privileged information—lawyer, client."

Iman, who was stretched out on the sofa in Donna Lee's office, cleared her throat. "Lecher man lose the house."

"That's not fair," Burma said, without much conviction. She was actually glad he had nowhere else to go. Now he'd have to stay at Graceland. And yet her conscience was clear. After all, she had tried to tamper with a witness so he would be able to keep his own house.

"What are you asking me for, anyway?" Donna Lee said, after re-arranging the icepack on Iman's head. "You live with him, don't you? That's what lost him that house, *Mrs.* Van Buren. Living with a married woman."

"For one thing, Miss Keely, I'm not married. And I'm not living with him, neither. You ask Mama. I got all my good clothes at her house. Right, Mama?"

Her eyes still riveted on Romans, Mrs. LaSteele pursed her lips tight as could be. "Sodomite, that's what my bible says."

"Thanks, Mama. Thanks for standing up for your child when the whole town's talking."

Except for Mr. Pickens, Burma might have added. He wasn't speaking to her, not since the trial ended two days ago. As if every-thing were her, Burma's, fault.

"Quiet!" Donna Lee said after futilely clapping her hands. Burma, Mrs. LaSteele, and the other Bible study member, Iman, had all started talking at once about the new spa tub the judge had or-dered Mr. Pickens to install in his ex-wife's house. And about a lavender salt at Bed, Bath, and Beyond.

"Let's stick to the Bible, if you don't mind. Mrs. LaSteele, do you have any idea what sodomite means?"

"Don't ask, girlie, and I won't tell."

"Well, she did ask," Burma put in. "And I'm fixing to tell. No,

Mama, don't put your hands over your ears. This you're going to hear whether you like it or not."

"Holy cats," Iman gasped from the sofa, "it's plain as day what it mean."

Stroking her administrative assistant's hand, Donna Lee said gently, "You called Mr. Pickens a sodomite the other day on the stand, Iman. What did you mean by that?"

The icepack leaked a trickle or two onto Iman's bronze cheeks. She had taken to the sofa a few minutes earlier when a mouse had whizzed across her huarache.

"Iman?"

"She meant he's a degenerate," Mrs. LaSteele put in. "Any man who has sex in a bush is by definition a degenerate."

Burma snapped the rubber band on her wrist. "You ask me, the real degenerate is someone who would film a man having sex in a bush. And besides, he wasn't having sex. He was just relieving himself because someone was hogging the bathroom."

"You hear that?" Iman demanded, tossing the icepack aside as she sat up. "She calls Iman a degenerate."

Burma stared innocently at the bulk that heaved itself from the sofa.

"Ladies, please," Donna Lee said, placing a restraining hand on her assistant. "Now, Burma, you should apologize."

"Me?"

"You're actually a sodomite yourself, aren't you?"

Blushing violently, Burma wondered how in God's name Donna Lee had found out her predilection for backdoor bunny love. This was outrageous, outing her in public like this.

"He who is without sin!" Burma said, gathering up her Bottega Veneta Hobo.

"Whoa, girl. I'm just trying to explain what sodomite really means. It's someone who doesn't welcome a stranger, a guest. That was the true sin of Sodom."

"No, Mum," Iman said. "It be the fag men. They what is going to bring down Sodom, and everyone in this Gomorrah here, too!"

"Amen," Mrs. LaSteele affirmed.

"I'm outta here," Burma said, yanking open the frosted-glass door.

Donna Lee pleaded for her to come back and finish the discussion. They'd never get through all that hummus without her.


## Vengeance Isn't Hers


"Then she called me a sodomite."

"Iman?"

"No, Donna Lee."

Mr. Pickens took a thoughtful sip from his mocha latte. They were sitting in wrought-iron chairs around a wicker table at Starbucks. The butcher who had been hacking snouts for a red-light special in the Piggly Wiggly meat department doubled as the Starbucks waitperson on Thursdays. Something reddish—surely not blood, one hoped—dripped from the mug he had handed Burma.

"Was it you, Bobby, did you tell her about me?"

Mr. Pickens's face glowed with a curious sympathy. Burma had never seen him look at her before with such genuine interest.

"No, I—Tell her what?"

"You know. My little secret." With becoming modesty she averted her gaze.

"You mean . . . Gee, Burma, they hadn't ought to stigmatize you like that."

"Oh, Bobby, it was awful, just awful. I'm never going back to Bible study again, never."

The tears that oozed were genuine, but also somewhat fun, refreshing. And as she buried her face in her arms on the table, was that his hand on her hair, lightly stroking it? She peeked to make sure it wasn't the butcher's.

"It's O.K., Burma. Don't let people like that upset you."

"She was using such awful language, too. 'Fags,' she said."

"Donna Lee?"

"No, that horrible assistant of hers." Raising her head from the table, Burma wiped a tear away. "I just wish she weren't Catholic."

"Iman?"

Burma nodded, then took a delicate sip. "See, Mama and Daddy brought me up real strict. We had to believe the pope was the whore of Babylon. Only now, the older I get, the more sorry I feel for whores."

His hand was on hers now, giving it a little pat. Right out in public, too, where any shopper might see them. Oh, she really couldn't get over how much good Bible study had done her. Ever since she had told Mr. Pickens about how mean they'd been to her, he had not only started speaking to her again, but actually volunteered to accompany her to Piggly Wiggly for their groceries. It had been the first time he had set foot outside Graceland since the divorce trial.

"Me, too," Mr. Pickens said. "I've always thought whores get a bad rap. Like sometimes you can understand why they might want to fool around with each other."

"What?"

"Well, considering how bad most men treat them, they might

look for affection elsewhere. All I know is, me, I wouldn't turn anyone into a pillar of salt for that."

"What's salt got to do with it?" Burma asked.

"Lot's wife. She turned into salt, didn't she?"

"That wasn't because she was a lesbian, Bobby."

"Of course not," he said, stroking her hand. "A woman who
makes it with another woman in front of a man, she's as normal as
apple pie."

"Carl Robert Pickens," she said, wrenching her hand free, "I may
be an old maid, but I'm no gym teacher."

He gave his mug a petulant shove. "But they called you a
sodomite, didn't they?"

"They called you one, too, buster."

"Me!"

"Don't act so surprised. You heard Iman call you that in court the
other day."

"In court I can understand. But in Bible study? Just what's going
on with you girls any way?"

Burma was about to object to his language—*girls*—until she suddenly remembered how old she was. It was odd how young this former boss made her feel, almost as if she were a mere chit at the old
Sonny Boy.

"I told you, Bobby, I quit. I'm not going back again."

The butcher suddenly loomed, wanting to know if they were
enjoying their beverages. Burma asked about the reddish streak on
her mug. He leaned over to peer at it, then shrugged and walked
away.

"Something's not quite right about Iman," Mr. Pickens said, after tapping a fingernail thoughtfully on a front tooth. "I don't like
the idea of her representing you tomorrow."

"She's not representing me. Donna Lee is."

"But she's on your side, Burma, a witness *for* you after testifying against me. Just what is she up to?"

Burma felt a sudden chill. She had forgotten that Donna Lee was using Iman as a character witness in Edsell Morone's lawsuit. And Burma had just called Iman a degenerate in Bible study! Oh, Lord, she'd really have to be nice to that woman again—and quick, too.

"Well, I hope the woman's got brains enough to know I'm not a racist." Burma blew onto her latte. "I might have called her a degenerate, but at least—"

"What? You called Iman a degenerate?"

"Yes, in Bible study. But look, Bobby, if I really were a racist, I'd have been too scared to call her a degenerate. It sort of proves I'm not."

She tried to sound confident. But the look he gave her didn't bolster anything but her growing doubt.

"Gee whiz, Burma, how can you be so dumb? Calling your own character witness a degenerate."

A spoon bounced to the floor as her hand came down on the table. "You want to know how I can be so dumb, Gee Whiz? I'll tell you. It's because I was trying to defend *you*. I was so mad she thought you were a sodomite, I completely forgot about my own case." She stood up so abruptly the table wobbled.. "Godamighty, I am dumb. Dumb for having you as a friend."

"Shouldn't we leave a tip?"

"For what, Bobby? The salmonella?"

Nonetheless, he did plunk down a dollar—of his own, too.

At the checkout line, after they had filled their cart with groceries, Mr. Pickens was back to his normal self. A slight glaze had returned to his eyes, which never met hers fully, always wandering off to see if something better might be around. Burma began to wonder

167

if she had been wise to squash his hopes about her own particular brand of degeneracy.

"Check that out, dog," she whispered with a nudge. A shapely woman in skin-tight pedal pushers was leaning over her shopping cart.

"What?" he finally said, too late. The leaning woman had disappeared into canned fruit products.

"Never mind."

"Never mind? I tell you, Burma, for a woman who's about to be sued for five million dollars, you're pretty relaxed."

"What do you want me to do, Bobby?" she said, handing the clerk her Winn-Dixie Bonus Club card. "Kick and scream all day long?"

"Ma'am, we don't take these," the clerk said, handing back the card.

"Why not?"

"This is Piggly Wiggly. We hate Winn-Dixie."

"Oh, sorry. See, Bobby, I am nervous."

"Huh?"

"Never mind."

## Reclaiming the Land

*H*ave you ever seen a squirrel look relaxed, taking it easy? Talk about paranoid. You love it to death, just want to pick it up and hug it, and what does it do, dart one way then the other, eyes bulging clear out of its head. Well, Mister, not everyone on earth is out to eat you. Chill out.

Thus were Burma's thoughts that afternoon while Mr. Pickens put away the groceries in Graceland's bisque Amana with ice-water dispenser. She was surveying the workmen's progress on the grounds, which seemed a haven for squirrels with scraggly, nonbushy tails. Was something lacking in their diet? she wondered. Or were they from a weak gene pool?

As she started to get up from the bench by the largest catfish pond, another thought made her settle back down again. Why wasn't Mr. Pickens more like these squirrels? Why did a man who had received so many neutering threats seem just the opposite of these squirrels? He never looked over his shoulder while he nibbled nuts. You never saw any muscles tensed and rippling under his fur, ready for action. And he hardly ever feinted in one direction to go another, not even when they played tag. (An article in the *Guns & Ammo* in her dentist's office suggested playing tag with a partner who had lost interest in sex.) At the Piggly Wiggly he had plodded calmly up one aisle and down another without the least fear, it seemed, of being grabbed by the balls. And all the time he had the gall to wonder aloud why *she* wasn't acting more nervous.

"Well?" he said when she returned from her inspection of the grounds.

"Well what?"

"Did the new pipe arrive yet?"

"No."

They had been waiting three weeks for the special-order pipes from Maine. When Edsell had wielded his pickax for the cross, you see, he had broken through an old sump tank. Sludge had leaked into the largest catfish pond, killing off the rare carp stocked by Dr. Schine. The leak had also upset the drainage system that shuttled rainwater off the property. One puddle was so deep now that a great blue heron had set up shop. In his lawsuit, of course, Edsell was claiming it wasn't the cross that had caused all these problems. These were existing problems that were blamed on the cross. That was how

169

the pond had poisoned him, left him with an amoeba that ruined his entire digestive system. He was not just lactose intolerant now, he also couldn't eat about a hundred other things, including wheat, broccoli, carrots, cabbage, romaine, or Three Musketeers.

"What's the problem?" Mr. Pickens asked.

The foreman had told Burma just a few minutes ago that the semi carrying the pipes had been in an accident outside Parsippany, New Jersey.

"Parsippany?" Mr. Pickens said, as he weighed a yam on the kitchen scale.

"Yes, Bobby, a chicken plucker ran into him."

"A chicken plucker?"

"Must you repeat everything I say?"

"Fifteen ounces," he said, taking the yam off the scale.

"Every time I'm with you, Bobby, I keep on forgetting you've got this man after you."

"What man?"

With a sigh she began to core an eye out of the yam. "The man that's fixing to make you a soprano."

"I need a towel. Where are all the towels?"

The freshly rinsed rutabaga in his hand dripped onto the slate flooring. Without even bothering to open the drawer with all the kitchen towels, he reached over and wiped the rutabaga on her fanny.

Outraged at being treated like a dishrag—she had just had her Redds uniform drycleaned!—Burma almost could ignore the electric delight that coursed through her, setting her very hair on end.

"Sorry, sorry," Mr. Pickens said after she demanded an apology that, on second thought, she really didn't want. "I was just trying not to get the floor wet."

"Don't you know that's a very sensitive area?"

"Yes, Mother, I know I'm not supposed to get water on your precious slate."

"My fanny, Bobby. I'm talking about my fanny."

She gave the area a little illustrative massage, but his eyes were on the floor.

"Whose idea was it to install slate that gets water stains? In a kitchen yet."

"Yes, I am nervous," he was saying a few minutes later after the yams and rutabagas had been weighed and labeled. "Why the hell do you think I'm living way out here in the middle of nowhere?"

Burma set the microwave for ninety seconds. They were both too hungry to wait for the yams and rutabagas to bake, so tonight they would have the frozen White Castle minicheeseburgers that Mr. Van Buren had won a year's supply of just before he passed away. (It was disgusting what good luck that man had. Why was it polite people never won anything?)

"The way you act, Bobby, it's not like a desperate man. I seen plenty of movies where someone was being stalked, and no one ever acted like you, going around yawning all day, scratching yourself in places a woman shouldn't ought to see, not unless he really means something by it."

Mr. Pickens stared blankly at the mayonnaise jar on the table.

"Lord, Bobby, just a minute ago I had to remind you that your life was in danger. You forgot."

"I didn't forget. I was weighing our tubers. And besides, you're the one got me into this mess. That's something I do try to forget. Otherwise, I couldn't live under the same roof with you."

Burma took a sip of the prune juice she couldn't finish for breakfast. "So that's the thanks I get."

"Yes, that's the thanks you get for advertising a cross that's stirred up even more threats against me."

"Now look here, Mister. I set up that cross to prove just the opposite, that you hadn't ought to be neutered for your beliefs."

"They're not even my beliefs, Burma. Wasn't me writing those letters to the paper. Why don't you take that thing down? Stop antagonizing folks."

"Can you manage a couple more burgers?" she said from the refrigerator, where she was extracting more frozen minis. "I'm afraid they might go bad before too long."

He shrugged. "No sense in wasting good food. Anyway, like I was saying, if you take that cross down, things might simmer down. I could move out and look for a place of my own."

"No, sir, that cross stays. I refuse to let those slimy perverts win."

"What perverts?"

"All the rich folk who pervert scripture, who twist it into a gospel of hate and privilege and vengeance. I'm sick and tired of perverts winning. It's about time real Christians rose up and took back Jesus."

With a sigh, Mr. Pickens smeared mayonnaise on his bun. "I swear, Burma, I wish you'd never started going to that Bible study. I liked you better when you were an atheist."

"It wasn't Bible study that brought me back to Jesus, Bobby. They like to drive me away."

"What the hell was it then?"

"You."

He went right on smearing, as if he hadn't heard. Yes, she had spoken softly, barely a whisper, but if he had cared to listen, he would have heard.

In a way, though, she was relieved that he hadn't. Why give him the satisfaction of knowing how he had wrecked her life? When he had turned down her marriage proposal six years ago and then married her ex-boyfriend's ex-wife, well, it had done her in. She had lost all her gumption.

That was when it had happened.

She had been in bed two weeks, unable to get up, when she felt his arms around her, his body pressed close. It was just before dawn, just before she was going to end it all with a bottle of her mama's St. Joseph's.

His head nestled against her breasts, a definite sweet weight. From the window came a breeze that stirred a tress of his hair, as dark and lustrous as Dr. Schine's. Somehow it was Mr. Pickens and not Mr. Pickens, someone far more glorious than either she or Mr. Pickens could ever imagine separately. But now between them, the same yearning scent of far cedars wafted him to her and . . .

"Did you say *me?*"

She blushed as she screwed the lid on the mayonnaise. "Yeah, right, you."

Her sarcasm worked. He shrugged.

"Mama never allowed jars on the table," he commented as she put the mayonnaise back in the refrigerator. "She said only low-class people do that."

Burma debated whether to leave the jar in the refrigerator or bring it back out to the table. Certainly she hadn't put it away to prove she wasn't low class. Why, oh why was that man always saying things that vexed her so?

That was the real reason, of course, why he hadn't married her. He thought she didn't have any class. Yet she was the one who had studied music appreciation in those night courses at St. Jude, three years in a row! Mr. Pickens didn't even know who Palestrina was, much less Ned Rorem. And *she* was the one who hated Elvis almost as much as Dr. Bierstube, her instructor, did. Mr. Pickens, why, he used to wear blue suede shoes in the seventies. This was the man who had the gall to tell her about jars on the dinner table.

"What's this?" he said, as the mayonnaise was plunked in front of him. "I don't need any more."

"Neither do I," she said, slamming the kitchen door behind her.

The sullen January air burned against her cheeks. In the distance the foreman's pickup kicked up a cloud of dust by the sump-tank sinkhole. He was leaving finally, after having done nothing all day but putter around with a surveyor's chart, spraying orange on the gravel.

From a rise bordering the largest catfish pond, she paused to survey the plastic cross Edsell had assembled. For some reason it was like seeing it for the first time. Already set, the sun yet managed to reflect some rays on a fleeting wisp of cirrus high above. In contrast to this tender glory the hollow plastic below seemed tacky as sin.

A groan escaped as she trudged on, determined to put as much distance as possible between her and that man. With each step the ivory columns became a little smaller. Yes, if she had to, she would hike clear to Massachusetts. She would find that man who had shaken up her life so, making her love and hope for the impossible. Peace on earth? Don't make me laugh, Big Bertha. The violent always win, always.

A pond overflowing with leaking sewage swamped the cattails where red-wing blackbirds once stalked their mates. To stay dry she had to make a detour. Emerging toward a stand of pines, she caught sight of an unfamiliar roof. Or was it a steeple there on the horizon? It was faint, though, so faint that she wasn't watching where she stepped. A metallic Mary Jane landed right on top of a crawdad castle.

They were her best shoes, these Christian Louboutin. After breaking a twig from a Chinese tallow, she scraped the soles. Then she was ready to forge ahead.

But the steeple wasn't there any longer. Squinting at the horizon, she began to wonder if it had simply been a play of light, the dusk catching a configuration of tree limbs to make them look man-made.

Shivering, wishing she had had the sense to put a sweater on before her grand exit, she turned back toward her mansion. Or what she thought was the mansion. Only now she saw the steeple again.

Though not a steeple.

Her steady pace broke into a jog. She was actually perspiring by the time the scent reached her—a delicate balsam, like something tasted with a flickering tongue.

Not a steeple. No. A pagoda.

Right here in her own woods.

Who had stolen onto her property to build such a thing?

The beams curved artlessly, without a hint of the maker. Richly textured, the cedar didn't seem treated at all. Yet it was smooth, dark as a blood stain. And as fragrant as if the wood had been freshly wounded.

A sweet anguish opened her arms. As she collapsed her great bulk of calories onto its planks—forgetting all, every injustice, every desire, every last yam she should have eaten instead—the temple embraced her.

## A Wet Stola

"O man, dear," Burma said, "I've been looking all over for you." The stony look was not encouraging. Nonetheless, Burma forged ahead. She was determined to apologize as fast as possible for calling Iman a degenerate the other day. After all, there was only

175

an hour before the woman would be taking the stand as a character witness.

"I must have phoned Donna Lee a hundred times this morning."

"Ten, fifteen, and twenty," the clerk said, doling out change to Iman's extended hand.

They were the only customers in Southern Auto. Burma had been searching for a leaf-blower silencer when she noticed Iman at the counter.

"Why you gawking at me, Mum?" The nip in Iman's voice could give a body frostbite.

Burma peeled her eyes away from the shotgun Iman had just paid for—a sawed-off shotgun that seemed somewhat illegal. "I was just . . ."

"Well, Mum?" Iman said as she headed for the door with her purchase. The clerk hadn't even bothered to wrap it. Iman was carrying it under her arm, cocked. And not a soul had asked her for an ID, much less a background check. Lord, she was wearing that outfit, too, the white smock with the turban—or rather, wimple. Not that she, Burma, had anything against wimples. Actually, in a way, it was nice that the clerk had made Iman feel so normal, didn't stare at her funny.

"You dropped this." Burma handed Iman the ready-made bow that the clerk had pressed to the sawed-off barrel.

"Keep it yourself."

"Really?" Burma smiled dimly at the yellow ribbons. "Mr. Pickens has a birthday coming up. I wanted to get him a silencer, but that clerk just looked at me like I was . . . For the leaf blower, you know."

"You want a silencer, Mum, get him a broom."

"Now that's thinking," Burma said, as sincerely as possible. "Iman, you always have such wonderful ideas."

Sleet pelted them as they stood uncertainly under the store's flapping awning. It was blowing sideways, this sudden upsurge of freezing rain. When Burma had gone into the store, there hadn't been a cloud in the sky, just a dull haze.

"If you contemplate an apology for calling Iman a degenerate, forget this."

"Oh, no. It's not that."

"Then you think Iman is?"

Although they were almost the same height, because of the wimple, Iman seemed to tower over her.

"Of course not."

"But you call me a degenerate, in front of my boss, too. And Iman about to take the stand as the character to witness for you."

"Well, just forget about the degenerate stuff," Burma said, nudging away the double barrel that was resting on her Marc Jacobs zebra–print Venetian satchel. "I was just upset because you called Mr. Pickens a degenerate. Take it from me, Iman, that man is no degenerate. I'd be very happy to report if he was."

"What?"

The wind was gusting so fiercely that at least half of Burma's apology was blown clear across Flat Avenue.

"Speak up, Mum!"

"You got an umbrella?"

"No!"

"My shoes, they're getting soaked!"

"Come on! We make a run for it."


Burma turned up the kerosene space heater in the assistant manager's office as high as it would go. Slipping out of her wet Louboutins, she said, "I don't mean to be nosy or anything, Iman, but why did you buy that shotgun?"

"It be illegal to ask me that. The attorney general say so."

"I see. Well, I happen to have a few rules of my own. Number one, only cowards use guns. If you just have to kill innocent creatures, then be a man and make it a fair fight. And number two, get that piece of sawed-off crap out of my office!" Remembering the upcoming trial, she added, "I mean, if you don't mind that much and all. Oh, hi, Mama."

Mrs. LaSteele tottered into the office on spike heels. "Shame, Daughter. I ought to wash that mouth out with soap."

Despite Burma's protests, Mrs. LaSteele was showing her solidarity with the defendant by wearing a matching mother-daughter outfit, the same cashmere sweater set that Burma had on. Although Mrs. LaSteele hadn't been able to convince her daughter to stick a chopstick in her hair, she had done the next-best thing. Mrs. LaSteele had removed a chopstick from her own bun.

"Just look at your Loro Piana, Missy. It's like near ruined."

"I don't care."

Mrs. LaSteele spoke over her daughter's head to the character witness. "She doesn't care. Isn't that mature, Iman? Five million dollars this girl's set to lose if she doesn't shape up, and she doesn't care."

"Mama, what are you doing?" Burma said as Mrs. LaSteele picked up the shotgun leaning against the hat tree.

Sighting along the truncated barrel, Mrs. LaSteele muttered, "This ought to do, Iman. Right fine. How much I owe you?"

"Mama, did you make this poor woman here buy this for you?"

Mrs. LaSteele adjusted a matching Loro Piana opera stola to cover her goiter scar. "Of course. Anyone who works for WaistWatch doesn't have to pay tax on firearms."

"But, Mama, she works for Donna Lee now."

"Still get the discount," Iman said, showing Burma the tax-free receipt.

"That's not right," Burma said. "She should pay taxes. How are we ever going to get decent schools if everyone pretends they're born-again fitness instructors?"

"You want decent schools?" Mrs. LaSteele said. "Then get your heinie over to Southern Auto and pay the thieving tax yourself."

"No, Mama. You take this thing back right now. You had no business buying one in the first place. Whatever got into you?"

Mrs. LaSteele hefted the shotgun to her shoulder again. "The Second Amendment, that's what. That Keely gal tried to deprive me of my rights. I'll show her."

"You never should've had a gun in the first place, Mama. If I'd known you had one in that house, I'd have stole it myself. Lord, don't y'all know how evil guns are? Here I'm giving away every last cent to stop violence and my own kin's setting there aiming right at me. I'm waiting, Mama—either shoot or get off the pot."

"Don't pay her no mind, Iman," Mrs. LaSteele said, as she wiped both barrels with a lace hankie. "She just doesn't have a boyfriend, makes her real nasty."

"I've got more boyfriends than you'll ever have, Mama."

Mrs. LaSteele and Iman exchanged a pitying look, which wasn't lost on Burma.

"Just what boyfriend did you ever have, Mama? And you can't count Daddy neither. He's your husband and he's dead. And you, Iman. I've never seen you with a man, much less a boyfriend."

"As for me, Daughter, I happen to have stepped out just last night with Judge Brown. We took in a double feature at the drive-in. And Iman, she can't have a boyfriend, can you, Iman?"

"No."

"Unlike some people I know," Mrs. LaSteele said, patting the witness's hand, "she just happens to be married."

For the first time Burma noticed the modest gold ring almost hidden by the ample flesh of Iman's fourth digit. Well, it made Burma just furious. Her mama was right, everyone in the entire world was married—except her.

"I'm sorry, Iman. I didn't know. It's just that, well, I've never heard you mention a husband before."

"Oh, she's mentioned him, Daughter, she's mentioned him plenty."

"Would you keep out of this, Mama?" More sweetly, she said to Iman, "I'd really like to meet him sometime. Maybe we could get together for a drink after court today. What about it? My treat."

"Daughter, please. He's in Rome, her husband. She's a religious."

"What? Iman, you're a nun?"

"No, Mum, I be a corporal in the Daughters of Chastity. We are wed to Christ Triumphant in the person of His Holiness the Prefect of the Supreme Sacred Congregation of the Roman and Universal Inquisition."

Bobby-pinning a wisp of Burma's hair in back, Mrs. LaSteele said, "She means the pope."

"No, Mum, we serve the Prefect, Cardinal Bauer, my husband in Christ Triumphant."

"Whatever," Mrs. LaSteele said through her bobby pins, "that girl is married."

"My husband," Iman went on, "he do not recognize Benedict's authority. Benedict have a shipwreck in his education, run up against the coral reef of liberalism. He do not understand Aquinas. And he give the Eucharist to the infertile, sexual-active couple."

"Queers," Mrs. LaSteele glossed.

"No, not fag men," Iman corrected. "A man and his wife in they sixties, a talking head on the Fox."

"Well, bless his heart," Burma mused aloud. "Anyway, I'm not having this thing around here."

She lifted the shotgun off her tea tray, where it had been lodged while Mrs. LaSteele lined up more bobby pins in her mouth.

"You'll have to take it back to Southern Auto, Iman. I'm sure your husband would be ashamed of you, buying a thing like that."

"No, Mum, I be a defender of the faith, and the faith be under siege, right here in St. Jude parish."

"Oh, come off it. The only thing under siege in this parish is the ACLU."

"Daughter," Mrs. LaSteele said, "that priest at Our Lady, he'll stop at nothing. After that cross he tore down at Graceland, it'll be my gazebo next."

Yes, it had been Mrs. LaSteele who had built the pagoda in the woods behind Graceland. Burma had thought the workmen were there fixing the drainage system. That was why no progress had been made after so much time.

Iman nodded. "Mama be right."

"How can she be right, Iman? She's a First Baptist who's built a shrine to herself, a goddamn pagoda."

"It's a gazebo, Missy, where I mean to drink me some green tea and mediate."

But there was an altar there. Burma had seen it with her own eyes. It had a photo of Mrs. LaSteele, what Madama Butterfly might have looked like some sixty years later, minus the suicide. Beneath the photo was a stick of incense, wafting up its reverence.

"Mama, I done told you I don't want any of your First Baptists on my property—I don't care how short they are."

"But Dr. Schine's the one, daughter, he's the one told us to meet there without him. And I'm not going to disobey the boss of this establishment." She rapped Burma's desk with a chopstick she'd had up her sleeve. "No, Ma'am, especially after he told me it was *my* shrine now and *my* congregation."

Burma looked to the ceiling for help. Still in Massachusetts, Redds's manager nevertheless continued to make life difficult for her

181

in Tula Springs. He had indeed encouraged Mrs. LaSteele to hold Small Is Beautiful tea parties in the gazebo. From New Hope he mailed her pamphlets and books that she kept locked in the cherry-wood ark on which the incense sat.

"Oh, for heaven's sakes, Mama, I'm the one who hired Dr. Schine and I'm not going to—"

"Look!" Mrs. LaSteele pointed at the clock on the wall. "We got to get a move on, girls. Burma, you sure you won't let me put just one in your hair?" She waved a mother-of-pearl chopstick to tempt her. Burma ignored her.

"Iman," Mrs. LaSteele said, retrieving one of the witness's huaraches, "don't you have anything more normal to wear?"

"Leave her alone, Mama, she looks fine."

"But that turban, Burma. You know that won't sit right with Judge Brown."

"Don't listen to her," Burma said as she held open the door for Iman. "Your wimple looks real normal to me."

## Witness for the Defense

Although Burma had been appalled to learn that her mother had gone to a double feature with Judge Brown, she felt a little better about the whole thing after the bailiff said, "All rise," and the judge sauntered out and gave her, Burma, a little wave. Uncertain about courtroom etiquette, Burma didn't really wave back from the defendant's table. Just wiggled her fingers a little in the frigid air of Room 116.

At seventy-five, Judge Brown was considered one of the best-looking legal minds in St. Jude Parish, a real catch, except for the fact that he was still married. Mrs. LaSteele used to be his Sunday school teacher at First Baptist, so surely, Burma mused, there couldn't have been any hanky-panky at the drive-in. Even if Judge Brown's wife weren't in a coma, the judge surely couldn't be attracted to someone eleven years older who used to flatten beehives in Sunday school to show what the Dead Sea did to your hair.

Just as Burma was about to smile pleasantly at the plaintiff, Edsell Morone, so that the jury could see she was not a mean, vindictive person but a Christian who could forgive this two-bit slimeball for making her use up her vacation days in February, Mr. Harper let out a yelp. "I object!"

Why, the trial hadn't even begun and he was objecting.

Donna Lee gave Burma a wink as she strode back from the judge's bench, where she and Mr. Harper had been conferring with His Honor.

"What's wrong?" Burma whispered.

"Nothing," Donna Lee said, fingering the cameo brooch that made her look as prim as a schoolmarm. Across the aisle Mr. Harper, who was representing Edsell, glared at the brooch like it was a cockroach in need of a good stomp. Poor Mr. Harper looked so nice, too, with a polo pony on his tie and his hair real full and shiny, not flat at all. It was a shame he couldn't put on a more pleasant demeanor.

Sotto voce Donna Lee explained to Burma that Judge Brown had agreed to hear Iman's testimony first, since Iman had a dental appointment at three. That meant the PowerPoint presentation Mr. Harper had prepared on the effect of untreated sewage in a young man's intestines would have to wait.

"Do you swear to tell the truth, the whole truth, and nothing but the truth, so help you, God?"

"No." Iman took the Bible from the bailiff, opened it, and read. "Matthew 5:34: 'Swear not at all; neither by heaven . . . nor by the earth. But let your communication be, Yea, yea; Nay, nay; for whatsoever is more than these cometh of evil.'"

"All right," the judge said. "That's enough."

"Yea," Iman said, occupying her seat with a little flourish of her handkerchief. Actually, it was not a handkerchief, but a Loro Piana. Burma had given it to her as a keepsake just before they had shoved open the double doors to the courtroom. "Yea."

After some lengthy preliminaries establishing Iman's credentials as a character witness for Burma, Donna Lee asked a question that gave Iman pause.

"No," she finally said, "I do not think Mrs. Van Buren be Christian."

Donna Lee visibly blanched. "Well, moving right along, let me ask you—"

"No, Mum, we stay. Mrs. is about as strayed from basic Christian doctrine as Benedict is."

"Benedict who?" Judge Brown asked. "Arnold?"

"Your Honor," Donna Lee said, "if you don't mind, the witness has already explained Benedict is the pope."

Burma felt sorry for Judge Brown. He had dozed off during the preliminary questioning, when Iman had told the court about the Daughters of Chastity's investigative work for the prefect of the Inquisition, Cardinal Bauer.

"Young lady," the judge admonished Donna Lee, "I know good and well who that man is. I was just testing the witness to make sure she didn't come here with any prejudice against those papists. That pope they got is an A-one patriot who helped us defeat those liberal swine, same as Miss LaSteele over there."

He smiled at Burma, who tried her best not to look confused.

"Proceed."

"Your Honor," Iman said, "no A-one patriot would pay four hundred dollars for foreign trash like this"—she waved the damp Loro Piana—"when the schoolchildren minorities go hungry for breakfast right here in her town."

"That was Mama!" Burma said, getting to her feet. "She bought that thing off eBay so we could match! From a sheriff's auction in Mississippi!"

Mr. Harper jumped to his feet. "Objection, Your Honor!"

"Order! Order!" The gavel banged vigorously. "Sit down, Mr. Harper."

"What about her?" Mr. Harper said, pointing at Burma.

Burma stood another moment, defiantly, and then sat back down of her own accord.

Here she would have appreciated a packed courtroom, murmuring their admiration. But for some reason, aside from the stenographer, only a handful of people had bothered to show up. Must be the pep rally drawing folks away.

"Proceed," Mrs. LaSteele prompted from her front row seat.

"Thank you," Iman said. "Your Honor, no one who shacks with a married man can be A-one patriot, much less a Christian. Yet this do not matter here. Cardinal Bauer can use anyone, even the basest degenerate, to accomplish His Blessed Congregation's will."

"How so?" Mrs. LaSteele asked.

"Your Honor, if you don't mind," Donna Lee said, "would you instruct her to let me direct the questions?"

"Proceed," the judge said, after issuing Mrs. LaSteele a warning.

"Her cross, Mrs. Van Buren's," Iman went on, "it be used to glorify Our Blessed Congregation's mission on earth. As I say earlier, Your Honor, I be sent out from Alexandria to bring the sheep back into the fold."

"Members of the jury," Judge Brown said, aiming his stare at Bubba Pascal of Pascal Mitsubishi and Hummer, who was knitting a throw for his tight end, "that thing the witness has on her head"—he pointed with his gavel—"I don't want you getting any prejudice against it, hear. It's what ladies wear in Alexandria, which is way yonder in Egypt. It's the most normal thing you'll ever see there."

"Your Honor," Donna Lee said, "the witness is not from Egypt."

"No, Your Honor," Iman said, straightening the wimple his gavel had accidentally set askew. "Iman is not. The Daughters' Fifth Squadron is based in Louisiana—Alexandria, Louisiana."

"Then why the hell you got that towel on your head?"

"Me, Your Honor?" Iman said. "What on my head be regulation uniform. What be your excuse?"

"Beg pardon?"

Burma blushed, as if she herself were wearing a rug, not the judge. Good thing Judge Brown had such a bad memory about anything going on from the waist on up. He didn't even get mad at Iman.

"Never mind," Iman went on, "nothing Your Honor say make me feel any worse about this town. I sent on missions everywhere, clear to Sioux City, but never do I encounter such corruption and subversion of the congregation's sacred doctrine."

"Can you give the court an example?" Donna Lee asked.

"Your Honor, I object," Mr. Harper said, getting to his feet. "What possible revelance can all this have to my client's case? Mr. Morone here has been waiting patiently for one iota of fact that bears on his intestines and—"

"Sit down," Judge Brown said.

"I haven't even had a chance to make an opening statement and—"

"One more peep out of you, Harper, and you're in contempt. Proceed."

Iman cleared her throat. "The priest from Our Lady vandalize

Mrs. Van Buren's property last night. He yanks up her cross, Your Honor, the one that honors all the victims of the rhythm method."

Burma felt hot all over, prickly. Of course, it was she who had pulled up the hollow WalMark cross at Graceland. She had decided that it wasn't really necessary to be tacky in order to be a Christian. Furthermore, she wasn't going to force Mr. Pickens to stay with her. If he stayed, it should be of his own free will. However, this was not the time to let Iman know about her change of heart.

"Good for him," the judge said. "Anyone who's against the death penalty should be forced to see his wife violated by a red-blooded all-American patriot."

"But Mr. Pickens doesn't have a wife anymore," Mrs. LaSteele said. "So you should stop phoning him, Brownie. Stop threatening to have him spayed."

Burma sighed. She should have known. It was Judge Brown who'd been threatening Mr. Pickens. And all this time she had thought it might be Edsell.

"No one listen to that woman over there," the judge said, point ing his gavel at Mrs. LaSteele. "She's a nut case. Proceed, Mrs. Iman."

"Imagine a consecrated priest of the One, Holy, Catholic and Apostolic Church yanking up a cross, Mum."

"You seen him do it?" the judge demanded.

"Your Honor, I don't have to see to believe. I have faith that he did it."

"Your witness," the judge said to Mr. Harper.

"Wait, Your Honor." Donna Lee said. "I'm not through with her yet."

"Proceed. And you, Harper, sit your ass down."

"Now, Iman, could you please explain to the jury how you know it was the priest at Our Lady who vandalized Burma's property?"

"Indeed," Iman said as she folded the stola into a neat triangle. "Shortly after I arrive from Alexandria, I receive the Sacrament of Penance. I kneel behind the grill that the father make optional. Then I confess. I tell him I been using a device for three years to prevent the pregnancy."

"What the hell?" the judge muttered.

"Your Honor," Donna Lee explained, "the witness was simply obeying her general's orders. She was probing Father Mike, acting as part of the Holy Inquisition. She actually hadn't been using a device herself."

"Of course not," Iman said. "So I ask him, what I should do. I tell him I do not want any more of the children in my life. I am not a rich lady and I have six already. Well, Father Mike say it be between my conscience and I. He tell me not to worry what they say in Rome. God do not see this as bad sin. I have nothing to repent. I try to tell him I feel very bad about disobeying the Curia, especially His Holiness the Prefect. But he keep on saying, let it go. Get on with your life."

"And then?" Donna Lee prompted.

"And then a week later, I go back. I confess behind the screen again. I tell him I in love with a woman, a female woman. I tell him we move in with each other, make a nice house together. Well, Your Honor, Father Mike ask me if I love and respect the woman. Then, before I can answer, he tell me God be Love. Well, this too much for Iman. I knock that screen down and give Father Mike shock of his life. I shake the recorder in his pretty little face. Fool, I say, this here will defrock your sweet ass for good."

"Let's hear those tapes, girl," Mrs. LaSteele said. "Let's hear what those RCs are really up to."

"The tapes been shipped with prefect's seal to Alexandria," Iman said, as Judge Brown ordered the bailiff to remove Mrs. LaSteele from the courtroom.

"Hold your horses," Mrs. LaSteele said to the bailiff, who did just that, probably because of the sawed-off shotgun that peeked out from beneath her capacious Loro Piana stola. Burma could have kicked herself for not searching her mama before entering the courtroom.

"You listen good, Judge Hormel Brown," Mrs. LaSteele went on. "You could have got yourself a first-rate wife if you had played your cards right. All you had to do was scare off Pickens like I said so the coast was clear. Then you and my daughter could have been an item."

"Out! No one listen to that woman!"

"And you almost had Pickens out of the way, too. Another phone call or two and he'd have been history. And daughter would have stopped throwing her hard-earned money away on those sodomites who want to outlaw this baby here." She stroked the snub barrels jutting erect from her waist. "Daughter would have made you a rich man, Judge. All you had to do was trip over that extension cord plugged into your wife's respirator, just like what happened in the second feature last night. But you made one little mistake along the way, Brownie Boy."

"Bailiff, I order you to remove this loon from my courtroom!"

Her mouth dry as cotton, Burma tried to get her mother to stop aiming at the bailiff, who had drawn his gun. If she was going to aim at anyone, it should be Judge Brown, the one who believed in capital punishment. All this Burma tried to convey with frantic semaphors, her waves punctuated by a hoarse "Mama" or two.

"I order anyone with balls to take that gun away from her," the judge's voice came from behind the bench, where he was crouched. "What's your problem, bailiff? You a girl?"

"This baby isn't going nowhere," Mrs. LaSteele said, "till I get my constitutional rights back."

With a sigh Donna Lee grabbed her handbag and strode over to Mrs. LaSteele.

189

"Here," Donna Lee said after fishing around in her handbag a moment. The revolver emerged, the one Mrs. LaSteele had bought to help the Baptists buy a new organ.

"All right, Your Honor," Donna Lee said after the exchange had been made. "You can come out now."

The toupee with the neatly permed auburn wave appeared first. Then the judge himself emerged more fully as Mrs. LaSteele slipped the revolver into her purse. Donna Lee set the sawed-off shotgun down on the defendant's table, where it lay peacefully atop a deposition about Godzilla Glue's adhesive strength.

"Vernon, hon, tea Wednesday at four, my shrine," Mrs. LaSteele said to the bailiff, who, being an immoderately compact First Baptist, had put away his gun even before being called a girl.

"As for you, Brownie Boy," Mrs. LaSteele said, turning toward the bench. "Of my own free will I'm leaving this stinking courtroom of yours. Don't think I don't know how many folks you sent to the chair. What was their crime, boy? They were poor, that's what. Well, now, you touch one hair on my daughter's chinny chin chin and you'll see. What's good for the goose is good for the gander."

Clutching her purse, she walked down the aisle and out of Room 116, a free woman with all her rights intact.

*Part Three*

# My Cup Runneth Over

*M*r. Pickens poured.

"Enough!" she said as the tea overflowed onto the linoleum. "Don't you see what you're doing? You could've burned me."

"One lump or two?"

"Hand me a towel. No, not my good Fieldcrest. A paper towel." She dabbed at the tea on the floor. "Honestly."

It was still her office, the assistant manager's. But Mr. Pickens was now the manager of Redds. After Dr. Schine had officially sent in his resignation from Massachusetts, Mr. Pickens had applied for the job. Despite some misgivings, the head of Human Resources had hired him. But only after he had assured her in writing that "manager" didn't mean "boss."

"After work, Burma, we'll look at this one and this one."

She squinted at the houses he had circled in the classified. One of them was the Dambar house, twenty-two rooms. She had already told him it was way too big for them. But he goes right ahead and circles it.

"I won't have time this evening, Bobby. You go yourself and look."

"Why can't you go? This is important. We got to get settled. I can't stand another day in Renaissance Heights."

Divorced now, Mr. Pickens was temporarily housed in a trailer park until he and Burma found a domicile they could both agree on. The trouble was, he wanted something big and fancy. She was just looking for a certain homey comfort, something that wouldn't cost an arm and a leg to air-condition.

"Hand me one of them scones," Burma said when Mr. Pickens asked why again.

After buttering one end, she said, "For your information, I have a date tonight."

"What?"

"You heard me." She took a bite. Now that Mr. Pickens was officially single again, he didn't seem so worried about living with her, what folks might say. After all, Mrs. Pickens had already remarried—gone back to her first husband, Emmet Orney, who was already installed in her two-bathroom house. Burma believed it was the mood lights in the spa tub that had helped Emmet forgive Mrs. Pickens.

"How can you date when . . ."

"When what, Bobby?"

No, he hadn't asked her to marry him. And they never had done much of anything besides play tag. Why the hell shouldn't she date?

He took a sip of tea. "Who you going out with?"

Burma shrugged. "It's none of your business except that he's handsome and well-to-do. And a widower, too, just like me."

The Lenox cup rattled in its saucer as Mr. Pickens set it down on the office desk. "No, not Judge Brown. You got to be kidding."

She buttered the other end. "What's your problem? He happens to be the most highly sought after bachelor in a fifty-mile radius, Bobby. And I did try to say no. I told you I laughed in his face when he called the other day. But that man won't take no for an answer."

Burma was counting on Mr. Pickens to put his foot down, to forbid her to go out with that horrible judge. She really couldn't stand the sight of that rug with the wave in it.

"Burma, do you realize that man's wife just died yesterday!"

"He was in his chambers when it happened, Bobby. They can't

pin anything on him. Besides, he's had almost fifteen years to get used to it."

Mr. Pickens's eyes bulged, a good sign. He really was upset.

"You'd actually go out with the man who was threatening to neuter me?"

"He who is without sin." She rubbed her aching foot. "Besides, he did sway the jury in my favor. I didn't have to pay a cent to Edsell."

"Thanks to Donna Lee." His fist pounded the desk. "It had nothing to do with that judge. Donna Lee's the one proved the pickax did it when it broke through the sump tank. So Edsell himself was responsible for the amoeba he got in the catfish pond, not you."

"Well, anyway, he didn't arrest Mama. That's something."

"Great, so you agree to go on a date with someone because he didn't arrest your mother. I like that." This he said just before kicking the lawn chair he had been sitting in and storming out of her office.

Burma sat there a moment, basking in his rage. Surely no one would get that upset if he didn't care.

When the knock came on her door a few minutes later, her eyes welled up with tears. Yes, this was it. He was coming back to lay down the law. *Thou shalt not go out with a heathen judge who has sent the innocent poor to their death. I won't have it. You'll marry me, Burma LaSteele, or I'll know why!*

"Oh, it's you."

She tried not to look so disappointed, but couldn't help it.

Edsell didn't seem to notice, though. After a civil greeting, he pulled on his latex-free gloves and got to work.

"Sure is warm for this time of year."

"Edsell, it's July. What do you expect?"

"Open wide."

Her eyes shut tight, she did as told.

"By the way," he murmured, "I tried those cookies you recommended. Paul Newman's."

"Aah."

"They didn't mess up my plumbing."

"Aah-ghck qkkakk!"

"Course they're not really sweet as the ones I prefer. But I guess beggars can't be choosers. Every other brand sets my amoeba off."

"Kqqekck qeggga?"

Something was troubling her. She was trying to remember when she had recommended Paul Newman to him.

"Spit," Edsell said.

She leaned over and spit into the sink.

With a melancholy sigh, he handed Burma a plastic cup normally used for DayQuil. "Rinse."

As she rinsed, it came to her.

The tea tray was right by the sink. She picked up the silver tongs that had just put in three lumps.

"What's this?" Edsell said, blushing, as she handed the tongs to him. The bridal shower gift from Mrs. Pickens.

"Give them back to Mrs. Pickens. She did want them back, didn't she, Edsell?"

"Oh." He coughed. "You mean Mrs. Orney."

On his way out Edsell said, "Good day, Brother Bobby."

Mr. Pickens pressed himself against the doorframe, as if he were afraid of being contaminated by the former administrative assistant.

Burma ran her tongue over her canines. It felt so good. He had got that bit of cheeseburger out from last night.

"Let me get this straight," Mr. Pickens said, his face as fierce as Charlton Heston's when he was trying to act like Moses. "Here this guy sues you for five million and you hire him to floss you."

"He lost, Bobby."

"So? You should be furious at him. You should countersue for every cent he has. But instead you give him your good silver tongs."

"I feel sorry for him."

Edsell had lost the election for superintendent of Streets, Parks, and Garbage. The winner, Donna Lee, had banned all PreachOut America interns from city hall. Burma had donated enough to her campaign for Donna Lee to afford Iman as her assistant instead.

"Why those tongs, Burma?" Mr. Pickens demanded.

"Because Mrs. Pickens—I mean, Mrs. Orney—wanted them back."

Yes, Mrs. Pickens had had her flosser break into Graceland last August to retrieve the sterling silver tongs. This was back when Mrs. Pickens had been furious at the secret teas Burma and Mr. Pickens had been indulging in at Redds.

"He was the thief, Bobby. The guy who broke into Graceland when I was living there alone."

"And you feel sorry for that thief? You give him your best silver?"

"Jesus himself comes as a thief in the night, Bobby."

"Are you telling me that that slimeball who tried to ruin me is . . . ? That's blasphemy."

Burma gazed into his fury, rapt. He was not himself. Some strength, almost as dark as Dr. Schine's own lustrous hair, radiated from a body so unlike Schine's, and yet somehow . . . "Bobby, there's a little bit of Jesus in everyone, isn't there?"

"No, not in him. And certainly not in that judge you're planning to run off with tonight."

"But isn't that what 'love your enemy' means?"

"No sir, I won't. I just won't. It's too perverse. It's degenerate!"

"Shhh! We got a customer."

. . .

It was Mr. Harper. He needed a crowbar to pry the Astroturf out of Mr. Pickens's old office in city hall. Donna Lee said she wouldn't put up with that junk on her floor.

Although Redds didn't carry crowbars, Burma thought she had seen something in the janitor's closet he might use. As she rummaged among the mops and pails, he said, "Well, I see the IRS got Graceland after all."

"Yes, I'm glad."

"Glad?"

"At least your PAC didn't get hold of it. And I did owe a bundle. This actually cancels out the debt, you know. Now I'm free and clear."

She showed him a broom handle that might be used for prying. He said it was too round.

"And what's wrong with the IRS anyway?" Burma said as she went on searching. "Why shouldn't I help pay for schools and . . ."

"And the war."

"No, sir, I made my accountants in Baton Rouge specify that not a cent would go for WMDs."

"Good luck with that, Burma."

"You don't believe me?"

"Oh, I believe you said that, all right. Look, I'll just go to Southern Auto for the crowbar. Thanks."

Burma was musing about this at the cash register when the door chimes rang.

The turban was the first thing she noticed. She put on her distance glasses to make sure it wasn't Iman.

No, it wasn't. Definitely wasn't. And she had a walker, too.

There was an auction coming up soon. The IRS was going to sell Graceland. Why couldn't Burma bid herself? Yes, she'd get it back. And then if it was the last thing she did, she would give it to someone who had always gotten the short end of the stick, who had never had anything nice in her life.

But this time she would do it right.

"That thine alms may be in secret," Matthew 6:4.

She would get the firm in Baton Rouge to handle everything. No one in Tula Springs, not even this dear woman, whose every step seemed such an effort, would know.

But first she would have to figure out a way to get the woman's name. Without a name she was back to square one.

As she schemed to find a way—*a rebate, yes, a mail-in rebate for Snow White!*—the former manager seemed to smile down upon her from New Hope.